"Come on, I'll give you a ride home."

To his surprise, she stiffened. "No, that's okay. I'll call a cab."

"Meg, it's Sunday. There's hardly any traffic. Come on," he said more forcefully. "Get in the car."

Eventually, he had Meg and her suitcase reinstalled in the Avanti. But she wasn't happy. Nathan puzzled over her attitude all the way to her house. He hadn't even turned off the car engine when she opened the door and bolted for her gate.

Nathan swung out of the car. "Hey, wait up. You forgot your bag." But suddenly a child's voice distracted him.

"Mommy!" called a little girl with bouncing blonde curls, cherry-pink cheeks and the biggest cornflower-blue eyes Nathan had ever seen. He stopped in his tracks, puzzled—and then stunned. Because the child running down the walk was _____ and the woman s_____ !

Shannon Waverly lives in Massachusetts with her husband, a high-school English teacher. She wrote her first romance at the age of twelve, and Shannon's been writing ever since. She says that in her first year of college she joined the literary magazine and 'promptly submitted the most pompous allegory imaginable. The editor at the time just as promptly rejected it. But he also asked me out. He and I have now been married for over twenty-five years.'

VACANCY: WIFE

BY
SHANNON WAVERLY

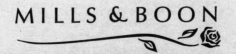
MILLS & BOON

To my grand-daughter, Victoria,
the original and incomparable "amazing Gracie".

*First published in Great Britain 1999
Harlequin Mills & Boon Limited,
Eton House, 18-24 Paradise Road, Richmond, Surrey TW9 1SR*

© Kathleen Shannon 1999

ISBN 0 263 81911 6

*Set in Times Roman 10½ on 11½ pt.
02-0001-52237 C1*

*Printed and bound in Spain
by Litografía Rosés, S.A., Barcelona*

CHAPTER ONE

MEG swerved into a parking space. She was going to be late. Second time in two weeks, too. Her heart thumped out a cadence that seemed to cry: Oh, no. Oh, no. Oh, no.

Leaping from the Escort, she hiked up her skirt, clutched her purse under her arm and bolted toward the factory, weaving through the crowded parking lot like a running back headed for a touchdown. Through the front door she flew, past the information window and across the foyer to the elevator. She hit the Up button, watched the light, muttered, "Come on, come on, come on!" and finally took the stairs.

By the time Meg reached the fourth floor, she was gasping for breath. On the top landing, she fell against the wall and took a moment to rest. The air trapped in the stairwell was close, a reminder of yesterday's unseasonably warm September day. Under her suit jacket, her blouse was glued to her back.

Suddenly a knot of resentment tightened in her chest. Why couldn't her mother-in-law have gone to the market last evening? Why this morning, when she knew Meg needed the car to get to work? It was so careless of her, as careless as last week's early run to the gas station "to save Meg a trip." Meg had only been at this job four months. Did Vera *want* her to get fired?

Immediately, guilt washed over her. She had no right to complain. Didn't the car *belong* to Vera? Wasn't she lending it to Meg out of the goodness of her heart? So why was she thinking such negative thoughts about the woman? Why was she being such an ungrateful shrew?

Pushing her large black-framed glasses up her nose, Meg glanced at her watch. Eleven past the hour. With a groan, she pressed on. With any luck Mrs. Xavier, her supervisor, would still be in the coffee room, unaware of her tardiness. Meg tugged open the heavy door and began her dash across the reception area.

She hadn't taken two steps, however, before she knew her goose was cooked—cooked, fried, baked and broiled— because standing at the receptionist's desk was the president and owner of Forrest Jewelry himself, Nathan Forrest. He looked up from a memo he was reading, and his eyes narrowed.

"Good m-morning, Mr. Forrest," Meg stammered, but since she'd lost her breath again, her words came out a dying gasp.

"Ms. Gilbert." He nodded curtly. Such a small gesture, yet she felt she'd been rapped across the knuckles. Face aflame, she continued on toward the business office.

At long last, luck fell in her favor. Mrs. Xavier was indeed in the coffee room. Of course, the other office workers noticed Meg's late entry, but they merely bid her a good morning and expressed concern that something had happened to her.

"Car trouble," she said, stretching the truth a little. Then she turned on her computer and was soon absorbed in the assignment she'd been working on at closing yesterday.

Two hours passed. Meg finished that task, and Mrs. Xavier gave her another, something new. She was always giving Meg new work. It almost seemed as if she was testing her, trying to gauge her limits.

Meg was just beginning to feel comfortable, just beginning to think there'd be no repercussions from her arriving late, when she glanced up from her computer and saw Mr. Forrest standing in the doorway staring at her. Frowning, actually.

Oh, hell, she thought, dread coursing through her even while she continued to type. She couldn't lose this job. She had financial responsibilities. She didn't *want* to lose it, either. It was the best thing that had ever happened to her, aside from Gracie, of course.

Meg's heart pounded as, from the corner of her eye, she saw Mr. Forrest push away from the door and start her way. Too soon his shadow eclipsed the fluorescent light falling on her keyboard. Too soon his clean blunt-filed fingertips rested on her desk. She looked up and forced a smile. "Yes?"

"Can I see you in my office, Margaret?"

Her mouth dried. Fumbling with the buttons on her suit jacket, she rose. Her co-workers' sudden silence accompanied her as she passed their desks. Oh, hell, oh, hell! she thought again.

She followed her employer across the reception area, with its tall, artfully-lighted glass cases displaying examples of Forrest jewelry, into his private suite. Unlike the reception area, which was tiled in gleaming faux-marble, Mr. Forrest's office was carpeted in deep sapphire plush, the very same shade as his eyes. The walls were cream, a perfect foil for the gracious eighteenth-century reproduction furniture he favored. Behind his mahogany desk a large window overlooked the city of Providence, capital of Rhode Island and center of the jewelry industry in the northeast United States.

Meg had been told that four years ago, when Mr. Forrest took over the factory from his father, he'd done a thorough renovation of this top floor. One could hardly tell that three levels of busy manufacturing were going on below. Here on the fourth floor, the designers worked at their drawing boards in skylighted quiet, the clerical staff tended to the business end of things, and Nathan Forrest oversaw the lot from a centrally located clutch of offices.

"Have a seat, Margaret," he said, rounding his desk. Meg lowered herself carefully into a wing chair, sitting straight and folding her hands in her lap.

He swiveled his own comfortable-looking leather chair to face her and gave her a direct, protracted look. As usual the force of those penetrating sapphire eyes threatened to knock a hole the size of Texas in her composure. As usual she thought she handled her reaction to him well, gazing back with a calm impassivity that belied the infuriating crush she had on him.

It was hard not to have a crush on the man. He was a dream. He had the sophisticated good looks of a Pierce Brosnan and the flawless fashion sense of a top Italian designer. He was charming and personable, as well. The *Ocean State Journal,* a regional monthly, often ran photos of him at social and political events, usually with an elegant heiress or fashion model by his side.

As if his looks and social popularity weren't enough to bowl over the average female, Nathan Forrest was also a major new force in the jewelry industry. The merchandise that bore his name, while just costume jewelry, was the very finest of its kind in quality and design. He'd made it so under his short dynamic tenure and as a result had already quadrupled the volume of business.

Even in his everyday dealings at the plant there was much to admire. He worked as hard as anyone, routinely putting in ten- and twelve-hour days, and because he kept himself involved at every aspect of production, he was as likely to be found experimenting with designs in the creative department as helping a foreman in base-metals repair a piece of broken machinery.

In addition, he traveled widely; he sailed, flew his own plane, played polo and was fluent in three languages.

Yes, it was easy to have a crush on Nathan Forrest. It was also entirely harmless, Meg thought, as harmless as having a crush on a rock star or film idol since he was just as distant, just as unattainable. Not only did he exist on a whole other plane socially and economically, he also made it a strict policy to keep romance out of the workplace.

"Mr. Forrest might have an active social life outside of work," Mrs. Xavier had warned Meg soon after she was hired, "but here he's all business. He even frowns on co-workers carrying on romances. Says it cuts down on efficiency and concentration. You start wasting time flirting with him or trying to get him interested in you, you're likely to find yourself out on your ear."

That policy was fine with Meg. Currently she had neither the time nor the inclination for a romance, office or otherwise. She had too many other affairs to juggle. And as far as Mr. Forrest was concerned, she was a level-headed person. She knew the difference between reality and fantasy, and she valued her paycheck far too much to get the two confused.

"Margaret, I have a favor to ask of you," he said now.

Meg blinked and made an effort to focus. A favor? He'd called her in here to ask a favor?

"This weekend," he continued, "I have to go to my parents' house down in Bristol. The family'll be celebrating my father's birthday on Saturday."

He wasn't displeased because she'd been late? Wasn't about to chew her out? Meg sagged with relief.

"Gathering at the farm on the first weekend of September has become something of a tradition with us," he added. "A combination birthday party, family reunion and send-off for the summer."

"Sounds very nice."

"Mm. It is." But reservation undercut his response. "Actually I'd prefer to stay here and work on the spring catalogue. Final copy and layout changes have to be at the printer's Monday if it's to be done in time for the first fall trade show. But since I can't, I plan to do the next best thing—try and work there. That's where you come in, Margaret.

"I've never asked you to work a weekend before. I understand you made that a stipulation when Mrs. Xavier hired you—no overtime. But this weekend I was wondering if you'd make an exception and agree to come along as my assistant."

Meg's eyes snapped wide open. "Me? You want me to accompany you to your family's get-together?"

"Yes." He sat back in his chair, shoulders relaxed, legs crossed ankle-over-knee, a man comfortable in his body as well as in his world. Sunlight angled across his head, setting off haloes in his silky black hair. "We'd be leaving tomorrow night and staying over until Sunday, so if you…" He paused when he saw her shaking her head. "What's the matter?"

"I'm sorry. I can't." She hated to refuse him. She was trying so hard to establish herself as a reliable and conscientious employee. But weekends were reserved for Gracie.

"If you're worried about it becoming a habit," he added, "rest assured, it won't."

"No, it isn't that. I…I already have plans." Meg noticed a faint shadow of irritation enter his expression. He probably thought she had nothing important to do once she left here. He probably thought she was selfishly choosing her leisure over work.

But then, he didn't know about Gracie, did he? And why should he? No one else at the factory did, either.

Before coming to Forrest, Meg hadn't worked in over three years. She'd quit her last job during her pregnancy and had spent the rest of that time at home with her daughter. Finally, with her mother-in-law retired and able to baby-sit, Meg had decided to return to the business world— only to find landing a job unexpectedly difficult.

Although interviewers had been impressed with her skills, she'd felt their interest cool as soon as she mentioned she was single and had a preschool-age child. Although they never said anything outright—that would've been against the law—she knew what they were thinking. A preschool-age child meant above-average absence from work due to illnesses, unreliable baby-sitters and childhood's other little inconveniences. Moreover, those absences increased significantly when the employee came without spousal backup.

Meg had tried reassuring them that she came with no such problems. Her mother-in-law was her baby-sitter; she lived at the very same address and was "on call" nearly twenty-four hours a day. But still no offers came through.

After weeks of pounding the pavement, Meg decided to experiment. On her next interview she'd refrain from divulging she had a child, just to see what happened. All she'd wanted was a chance to prove herself. Once she had, she'd gladly admit what she'd done. Her next interview happened to be at Forrest.

Lying had seemed a simple enough ploy four months ago. Meg had even believed that once she told the truth, people would admire her for doing her job as well as she did while being a single parent.

She'd been stupid. How could she tell the people she worked with she'd deceived them? What would Mrs. Xavier think of her, holding back such fundamental information all this time? And what about Mr. Forrest? How much trust would he place in her then? The worst part was, the longer she waited, the bigger her lie grew and the harder it got to straighten out. She felt trapped in a web of her own making.

With a start she realized Mr. Forrest had just asked her a question. "I'm sorry. What did you say?"

"I asked if you're absolutely certain you can't work this weekend."

"Yes. I'm sorry," she repeated, wetting her parched lips with the tip of her tongue. "But surely someone else can go in my place. Mrs. Beeden maybe or Mrs. Hall." Both women had worked for him longer and were more knowledgeable of the business.

"No, not really. I prefer you on this particular assignment, Margaret. First of all, you're single and they're not. They have families to see to on weekends."

Meg looked down at her hands, feeling her lie spinning out.

"But more importantly," he went on, "in the few short months you've been here, you've impressed me with the way you work. You're remarkably diligent and efficient, Margaret. On top of that you're smart. You don't just type; I've seen you compose and edit, too. I'll need those skills this weekend when I'm working on the catalogue. I'll need your accuracy on the number pad, too, since the price list also has to get done."

Meg sat straighter, a smile of pride tugging at her lips.

"But the most valuable asset I see, especially considering this is a family occasion…" He paused, one finger over his lips while he stared at her thoughtfully. "I trust you, Margaret. You have a maturity that's rare for someone your age. You're quiet, sensible. You don't waste time in idle talk. You keep your mind on your work instead of on other people's business. What I'm trying to say is…"

She supplied the words for him. "That I won't talk about the weekend when I return?"

He smiled, causing the most adorable dimple to appear in his right cheek. "Precisely."

Meg was surprised he'd noticed that about her. She hadn't thought he was aware of her at all. She was a very small cog in a very big wheel, after all, and he…well, he was the owner. Not just an executive. The owner. The president. The big enchilada.

"Not that anything scandalous is likely to happen," he added, his eyes twinkling as his smile broadened. Meg had to look away. He was simply too gorgeous for words. "It's just that I'd prefer details of my personal life to remain...well, you know...out of the pipeline."

Meg sympathized. In spite of his personable nature and busy social calendar, she'd always thought there was something defensive about Nathan Forrest, something that wanted to avoid exposure and remain hidden. Still, she couldn't see herself surrendering a whole weekend with Gracie just so people in the office wouldn't know what he ate for breakfast on Saturdays.

"I'd really like to help you, Mr. Forrest, but I can't. I...I have that prior commitment."

Apparently "no" was not an answer he was prepared to take. "Okay, I'll be honest. There's more to the weekend than work." He sat forward, closing the space between them and ratcheting up the pressure. "I also need someone who can help me out of a personal jam."

"A personal jam? Me?" Meg was thoroughly confused now.

"Yes. I need you as an excuse to...to avoid a certain unpleasant situation."

Meg pushed her glasses up her nose and frowned. "What do you mean?"

"Explaining is so awkward." He sighed. "I imagine you know I'm not married, right?"

"Ye-es."

"And you've probably heard I really enjoy my bachelor status."

Meg hesitated. If she said yes, would he think she'd listened to office scuttlebutt? Fortunately, he didn't wait for her to reply.

"Well, I do, and I fully intend to continue enjoying that status for at least the next five or six decades. The trouble is...my mother. To put it simply, Margaret, she thinks I should be married. Consequently, whenever she gets me on her turf, she shackles me with the unmarried daughter or niece or neighbor of one of her many, many friends."

"She arranges blind dates for you?" Meg's eyes widened. If ever there was a man who didn't need help getting a date, it was the one sitting before her.

"Yes. Well, not exactly dates, but it's obvious I'm expected to be their dinner partner or escort through whatever event we're celebrating with hopes that I'll continue seeing them beyond the event and eventually fall deliriously in love.

"But this weekend I don't have the time to put up with my mother's matchmaking schemes. I don't have the patience, either. With you along, I wouldn't have to."

Meg could feel her face warming. "Mr. Forrest, you aren't suggesting we, um...we let people assume..."

He stared at her, his brow furrowed. Then, "Oh, good Lord, no. I merely meant I wouldn't be able to entertain someone else if you were along. It wouldn't be polite to abandon you among strangers."

Meg burned with mortification. How could she be so stupid as to misunderstand his intent? As if anyone would ever believe he was interested in *her!*

She knew she wasn't homely, but she was hardly pretty, either. Plain was what she was, as plain as vanilla ice cream, as ordinary as the common wren. Her skin was medium-olive. Her hair and eyes were medium-brown. And at five-three and 113 pounds, her build was as average as average got.

Perhaps makeup would help the cause, but with a three-year-old underfoot, she didn't have time in the morning to fuss. A dusting of blusher, a stroke of lip gloss, and she was done. She kept her hair equally simple, too, tying it back in a neat low knot at her nape. Only the scarf or scrunchie encircling it changed with the day.

No one would ever accuse her of being a fashion plate, either. But then, that wasn't her intent. Rather, she aimed for a classic look, one that was neat, conservative and appropriate for the office. She was hardly the type of woman Nathan Forrest dated, and for her to even suggest the idea was so laughable she wanted to cry.

Gentleman that he was, he moved off the subject quickly and got back to business, naming a sum he was willing to pay her for her weekend labors.

"H-How much did you say?"

He repeated the figure.

"For two days' work?" Her heart was beating in her throat.

He nodded. "If you need time to think it over, you can give me your answer tomorrow, although tomorrow *is* Friday, and I was hoping to be on the road soon after we shut down here."

"Isn't the get-together on Saturday?"

"Yes, but I was thinking we might fit in an hour or two of work tomorrow night."

"And where did you say this farm was located?"

"Not far. Bristol. It's a great place, very relaxing. It even has some ocean frontage."

Meg felt her conviction weakening. She'd be paid a king's ransom to spend the weekend by the ocean? With Mr. Forrest, no less? It seemed like a dream on a silver platter.

Immediately she became disgusted with herself. She wasn't really thinking of accepting, was she? She'd promised to take Gracie to the zoo on Saturday.

Oh, but the money she'd be earning! What she could do with that money!

On the other hand was there a price on the time she spent with her daughter? Gathering all her strength, Meg said, "I'm sorry, but I still have to say no."

"If you're concerned about what clothing to bring…"

"No." She wasn't concerned because she was *not* going.

"Casual work clothes will suffice," he persisted, a man used to winning. "Maybe a pair of slacks, a dress or two. *And* I'll have you back by Sunday afternoon."

"That's all very nice but…"

"I realize that doesn't give you much time to recoup for work the next day, so, tell you what, Margaret, you can take Monday morning off with pay. How's that?"

It sounded too good for words. "That's very generous of you, Mr. Forrest. But I still have to decline."

Before he could come at her with another argument—and he seemed about to—she got to her feet.

"Are you sure you don't want to sleep on it?" He rose from his chair, too.

"Yes, I'm positive."

"Boy, that must be some date you've got."

Weighing the benefits of silence over honesty, Meg swallowed the words of explanation she so longed to speak. "Yes. It is," she said and let him think what he wished.

By five-thirty, Meg had negotiated her way from the manufacturing district through rush-hour traffic out to the working-class neighborhood where she and Gracie lived with the Gilberts. Actually they lived in a self-contained apartment over the Gilberts' garage. Most days it just felt as if they all lived together.

As usual, Meg felt a pang of guilt when her thoughts regarding her in-laws turned negative. Vera and Jay Gilbert had been nothing but warm and accepting from the day their son first introduced them to her.

She and Derek had met at an accounting firm in St. Louis

where they'd both worked. She'd been an eighteen-year-old office assistant, fresh out of high school and attending secretarial school at night. He'd been a senior at a college nearby, majoring in accounting and doing an internship at the firm.

They'd dated until his graduation in June, at which time he asked her to move back East with him. Since her Aunt Bea, her last tie to the area, had recently died, she'd agreed.

Things moved quickly after that. By nineteen, Meg was married and living in the cozy apartment Derek's parents had created over the garage purposely for them. By the age of twenty, she'd given birth to Gracie. That was without a doubt the brightest day of her life. By twenty-one, however, she'd also experienced the darkest—the day Derek died in a car accident and she became a widow.

Looking back on that desperate, grief-filled time, Meg wondered what would have become of her and Gracie without Vera and Jay Gilbert's help. She didn't have any family, nor any source of income or place to go.

"But *we're* your family," they'd said to her, astounded that she thought she'd have to move on, "just as you and Grace are now ours." They'd insisted Meg remain living over the garage rent-free. They'd also provided utilities, groceries and just about everything else Meg needed to survive.

They claimed that Derek's insurance policy, which had still listed them as beneficiaries, was covering expenses. But even Meg, as naive as she was, knew that ten thousand dollars didn't stretch *that* far.

But the gift she valued most was the love they showered on Gracie. They absolutely adored their granddaughter. They'd been devastated by Derek's death. He'd been their only child, the center of their universe. But in Gracie they saw a blessing, a spark of life left in the world to burn in the darkness created when he died.

ing of claustrophobia began to crowd her. Frustration tightened her chest. Despite everything the Gilberts did for her,
there were disadvantages to living with them, too.

Meg backed into a tight parking space at the curb,
switched off the engine and reached for her purse.

"Mommy!" Gracie called excitedly, running from the
backyard toward the chain-link fence that enclosed the
Gilberts' yard. She was wearing a metallic-pink prom
gown, hemmed to her size, and a lopsided crown made of
aluminum foil. Playing "dress-up" was one of her favorite
activities these days, one that Meg had indulged with frequent trips to the Salvation Army store.

"Hi, sweetheart." Meg climbed out of the car, her heart
flooding with joy at the sight of her daughter. Physically
Gracie was a beautiful child, with Derek's bountiful blond
curls, expressive blue eyes and roses-and-cream complex-
ion. Meg was used to strangers stopping her on the street
to compliment her on Gracie. "She could be a model,"
they often said, or, "She ought to be in the movies."

But as beautiful as Gracie was physically, it was her
personality and intelligence that really impressed people.
They marveled at this three-year-old's verbal skills and
were utterly charmed by her sociability. "She's gifted,"
was another comment Meg often heard. And, "There aren't
too many like her."

Meg was well aware of that, and while her daughter was
an unending source of wonder and pride to her, she was
also a source of worry. Meg felt burdened with a special
responsibility. How to best educate this gifted child, how
to handle discipline, what activities to expose her to, what
sports, what crafts, which parks and museums to visit,
which TV shows to let her see? Was she doing right by
Gracie? Was she doing enough?

Vera found her concerns amusing, if not absurd. "She's

a baby, for heaven's sake. Just let her play.'' Meg had learned to quit trying to explain herself. Vera didn't believe in books on child-rearing, and while Meg relied on common sense, too, she knew the value of expert advice.

Meg opened the gate and scooped Gracie up into her arms. ''Hi, sweetheart. Oh, I missed you today,'' she said, planting a bouquet of kisses on her daughter's pink cheeks. ''What've you been doing?''

''Playing princess.'' Gracie hooked her arms around Meg's neck and wrapped her legs around her waist. The gown rode up, exposing chunky multicolored sneakers on her sockless feet. ''I'm going to the ball tonight.''

''You are! Where?''

''At the castle. I'm going to dance with the prince.'' Gracie had been watching a lot of Disney classics lately. Maybe too many?

Meg got a better grip—the gown made Gracie a difficult bundle to hang onto—and started up the walk. ''And how are you going to get there?''

''My magic carpet.''

''Oh. I thought you were going to say your pumpkin coach.''

''No,'' Gracie said with sudden sadness. ''The pumpkin coach isn't working today.''

''Oh, that's too bad. What happened to it?''

''The carburetor broke.''

Meg's lips twitched. ''Just like Grampa's car last week, huh?''

Gracie nodded solemnly.

''Oh, well, at least you still have that magic carpet. Hey, can I go to the ball, too?''

Gracie's sadness vanished immediately. ''Oh, of course,'' she said, sounding totally adult. ''But you need to wear a gown.''

''Of course. And will I meet a prince, too?''

Uh-huh." Gracie's curls bobbed over her forehead as
she nodded. Her crown tilted. "But you can't chew gum
at the ball."

"No?" Meg had trouble suppressing a laugh.

"No. You can't pick your nose, either."

This time Meg lost it. Gracie did, too.

Vera looked up from a flower bed she was neatening.
She was a plump woman verging on fat, with round pink
cheeks, an upturned nose and short, permed, pinkish-blond
hair. "What's so funny?" she asked, looking slightly left
out.

"Oh, nothing much." Meg tried not to resent the
woman's habitual need to share every word she and Gracie
traded. "Any mail today?"

"Yes. I put it on your kitchen table."

Meg set Gracie back on her feet. "Anything from
Children's Circle?" She'd long since got used to the
woman checking out her mail.

Vera struggled to her feet, puffing and groaning. "Children's Circle?" She frowned as if she'd never heard the
name before.

"Yes, the preschool I've enrolled Gracie in."

"No, there was nothing."

"Hmm. That's odd. Classes are supposed to start next
week. The application I filled out said information would
be forthcoming." Meg chewed on her lower lip, then
glanced at her watch. "I'm going to call. Someone might
still be in the office."

"Are you sure you want to bother?"

"It's no bother." Taking her daughter by the hand, Meg
started for the stairs that climbed the rear outside wall of
the garage.

"I made a stew. Why don't you just come in for supper
and call some other time?"

"Thanks, but I already have a meal planned."

Inside her apartment Meg tossed her purse and jacket on the sofa, then went directly to the phone. While she waited for the call to go through, she opened the refrigerator and took out an array of plastic containers filled with leftovers.

"Children's Circle," a pleasant voice answered.

"Yes, my name is Meg Gilbert and I have a question about next week's classes?" With the phone tucked at her shoulder, she began to prepare a plate for Gracie. "I believe my daughter should be showing up for school on September ninth, but I haven't received any information yet."

"What's the child's name, please?"

"Grace. Grace Gilbert."

Meg slipped the plate into the microwave, then waited while the woman on the other end of the line shuffled papers.

"When did you bring in her application?"

"I didn't. I mailed it in." Actually, she'd had Vera mail it for her. Suddenly a feeling of dread began to spiral through her.

"I'm sorry, but I'm afraid I can't find any application for a Grace Gilbert."

Meg clutched the receiver in two hands. "Are you sure?"

"Yes. Positive."

"But I'm sure…" She swallowed. No, she was not sure. "Can I stop by tomorrow and fill out another?"

"I'm sorry. We have a quota, and the class is already filled."

Meg closed her eyes, searching for composure. "Can I call back in a couple of weeks to see if there's an opening? Maybe someone will decide to drop out."

"It probably won't do any good. We have a waiting list already. Maybe you can try again at the half year. That's about the best advice I can give you."

Meg f———ll———————up Thank you. I'll do that.''

Gracie's meal was done, and although Meg disliked having the television baby-sit for her, she turned it on and set the plate on the coffee table. "Honey, I'm going over to Grandma's for a minute. You have your supper, and don't move. I'll be right back. Okay?"

A moment later Meg was standing in the Gilberts' back doorway where she could keep an eye on the garage stairs. Jay Gilbert had just come in from work and was sitting at the dinette table having a beer. Like his wife, he was heavy-set, but unlike her he was quiet, a man who usually had nothing original to say. He just echoed whatever Vera believed.

Vera looked up from the stove, ladle in hand, her face crimson. "The application? Of course, I mailed it."

Meg glanced at Jay, who immediately lowered his eyes. "Well, Children's Cirlce never received it, and I'm beginning to wonder why." Normally she didn't speak so boldly, but this was the second time in a month something important she'd asked Vera to mail had gotten "lost." The first had been a credit application for a department store.

Vera resumed stirring her stew, her mouth tight. "I don't see it as much of a loss anyway. Why you want to send Gracie to a day care center is beyond me."

"It's a preschool, Vera, not day care. And it's only three mornings a week. We've been through all this already."

"And I still think it's a waste of good money when you already have the best baby-sitter there is."

"Yes, I appreciate how much love and care you give her. But this isn't about baby-sitting. It's about providing her a chance to be with other children. It's about her engaging in stimulating activities. The kids have such a good time there, plus they do all sorts of things that prepare them for kindergarten."

Vera rolled her eyes. "For years kids've gone off to kindergarten without preschool. I don't see what the big fuss is now. Heck, when I was growing up, we didn't even have kindergarten. We just went straight into first grade.''

"Yes, but they have it *now*," Meg said with straining patience. "Vera, tell me the truth. Did you really mail that application?"

The woman tossed down the ladle, splattering gravy. "I already told you I did. What more do you want me to say?"

Her husband took his beer and quietly slipped off to the living room.

Meg's lungs felt on fire, because if ever a person appeared to be lying, it was the woman facing her now. But how could Meg accuse her? It would be Vera's word against hers. If she pursued the issue it would only lead to an argument. She didn't want that. For everyone's sake, especially Gracie's, it'd be better to smooth things over.

"Okay. I'm just asking," Meg replied, raising her hands. "I just wanted to be sure before I put in a complaint with the post office." Which she had no intention of doing.

Back in her own apartment, she prepared a microwave meal for herself, then sat with it at the kitchen table. But she couldn't eat. Her throat was too clogged with emotion. Disappointment for Gracie, frustration, anger. She disliked admitting to that last feeling, but, yes, anger was there, too.

Dammit! Vera had no right to undo a decision she'd made regarding her own child. Granted, Vera had acted with their welfare in mind. She'd believed she could take care of her granddaughter better than anyone else. She'd also believed she'd be saving Meg money in the process. Still, she'd had no right!

Meg stared at her food, congealing on the plate, then closed her weary eyes. If she were to tell a stranger how she felt, he'd think she was crazy. Worse than crazy. Petty. Ungrateful. Spoiled. But the truth was, she could hardly wait for the day when she'd be able to move out. That was

why should ————— —— work, not just to begin paying her
own expenses, but also to start saving money so that she
and Gracie could get a place of their own.

Meg hated being beholden to the Gilberts—and, boy,
was she beholden! They'd given her so much. But her debt
went far beyond a matter of dollars and cents. All those
months of free rent, free utilities, free baby-sitting and car
usage now felt like installment payments the Gilberts had
made on her and Gracie's love and loyalty.

Of course Meg loved her in-laws, and of course she
would always consider them family. But did that mean she
had to remain with them forever? More and more, she believed that was what their generosity was all about.

They wanted their son's family where they could see
them, hear them and be with them at a moment's notice.
The ironic thing was that Meg understood their need. She
and Gracie were a direct, visible link to Derek, a vehicle
for keeping their son's memory vividly alive. However, understanding didn't make coping with the situation any easier.

Lately Meg had begun to find their efforts to keep the
past alive especially distressing. The Sunday dinners where,
inevitably, they retold stories to Gracie about a father she
didn't even remember. The evenings when they came over
for coffee and just happened to bring along old photo al-
bums. Even their incidental conversations included unre-
lenting allusions to their son. "If Derek were alive" began
so many sentences. "You're just like your daddy," was
another favorite expression.

Quite frankly, Meg had had enough. Although she'd
cherished her husband and would never forget him, she'd
grieved as long and as deeply as she possibly could.
Grieved…and healed. Now she wanted to move on. It was
time. Living in the past wasn't healthy for either her or
Gracie.

She wanted to get out, meet new people, make new friends, do different things. And, yes, it would be nice to start dating again, too. Although she was in no rush to find a husband, she hoped to eventually remarry someday. She wanted to create a real family life for Gracie, maybe even provide her a sibling or two.

But she didn't dare say what was on her mind to Vera or Jay. They wanted her to stay just as she was, their son's widow, like an insect caught in a droplet of amber for all time. It wasn't just her imagination, either. Lately she'd begun to notice how often Vera discouraged her decisions, even thwarted her efforts, whenever she was about to make a move that might take her in the direction of independence. What was especially frustrating was that Vera acted under the guise of helping her.

Meg could put up with certain annoyances—Vera's causing her to be late for work, for instance. But now Gracie was being hurt, and *that* Meg would not abide.

More than ever moving out seemed to be the solution to her problems. Her moving would be beneficial to the Gilberts as well. They'd grown too attached to her and Gracie, too dependent on them for their emotional sustenance. They needed distance, too. Once they realized Meg had no intention of cutting the ties that bound them, they'd relax and see their relationship in a more reasonable perspective.

But before any of that happened, before she could even start to search for an apartment, Meg needed to save some money—which meant she had to earn some first.

With a determined lift of her chin, she pushed up from the table and went to the phone. She'd planned to spend the weekend with Gracie. Time with her was the most precious commodity there was, and they got so little of it, now that she was working. But it was obvious what needed to be done. A sacrifice now would pay dividends later.

_____, meg picked up the receiver and
dialed the number for Forrest Jewelry. It was ten minutes
to six. Mr. Forrest might still be there.

On the third ring, someone answered. Meg would have
recognized that deep voice anywhere.

"Hi, Mr. Forrest? It's Meg Gilbert." Silence. "Margaret.
One of your office workers?"

"Oh, yes. Yes, of course."

"I've been rethinking your offer of work this weekend,
and…and I've decided to accept."

CHAPTER TWO

NATHAN placed the phone back on his desk and sighed with relief. He was going to get the catalogue pulled together after all. A minute ago he'd had his doubts, but now...

A sudden smile lit his eyes. He'd almost forgotten the other benefit of having Margaret with him. His mother's infernal matchmaking would be foiled!

Which reminded him, he really ought to call his mother. She had to be told Margaret was coming. He picked up the phone again and pressed the number for Beechcroft, his parents' farm in Bristol.

"Hello, Lucy?" he said to the housekeeper who answered. "Is my mother available?"

After a moment Pia Forrest came on the line. "Nathan, what a surprise!"

"Hello, Mother. How's it going?"

For the next ten minutes she told him. He'd forgotten that about her. He forgot nearly every time he called. Where other people responded with a simple, "Fine," she took the question seriously and told him all the latest happenings in her life.

"The reason I'm calling," he said, interrupting a tale of woes about a newly-developed hitch in her golf swing, "I'll be bringing someone with me this weekend. I hope you don't mind."

That brought her up sharp. "You're bringing someone? Here?" Nathan could almost feel her frowning. He hadn't brought a woman to the house in at least two years. Too often his guests had read more into those invitations than

he'd ever ~~meant~~ ~~~~ ever-hopeful family
had.

"Yes. One of the girls from the office." If his first an-
nouncement had perplexed his mother, this one stunned her
speechless. "I'm afraid I'm going to have to spend part of
the weekend working," he explained. "That's why I'm
bringing Margaret."

"Oh, Nathan! You aren't!"

"Aren't what?"

"Going to spend the weekend working."

"Yes. Part of it anyway. It can't be avoided. The only
alternative is for me to miss the weekend altogether, and I
know you wouldn't want that."

"No, of course not, but…"

"That's why I'm calling, to tell you about Margaret, so
you'll have time to prepare a room for her."

His mother sighed. "Is it really necessary that she
come?"

If he'd had any doubt his mother was planning another
matchup, it vanished with that question. "Yes. I'll never
get the work done otherwise. Why? Is putting her up going
to be a problem?"

"No, it isn't that." Pia hesitated before confessing, "It's
just that, well, I've invited a charming young woman who's
looking forward to meeting you. But with you encumbered
with this girl from the office, well, that's just going to be
such an annoyance."

Yes, isn't it? he thought, smiling smugly. "I don't really
mind being encumbered with Margaret. She's a pleasant
enough person. Quiet. Unobtrusive. She won't be any
bother." At least he didn't think so. But actually, what did
he really know about her except that she was a terrific secretary? What she did after five was a mystery to him. He
didn't pry into the lives of his employees. What he knew,
they volunteered. Some volunteered a lot. Margaret vol-

unteered nothing. His knowledge of her, her skills and her character, came mainly from observation.

Suddenly Nathan felt a smile tugging at his lips. Although what he'd told her was true, that she'd impressed him with her work habits, Margaret Gilbert left a few other impressions on a man's psyche.

She was so...buttoned up. He'd never met a young woman more determined to hide her assets. With that severe hairdo and those stiff, unbecoming suits, she succeeded damned admirably, too. And those glasses! Why hadn't someone told her styles had changed a couple of decades ago?

In a way, though, how she dressed was part of her charm, because beneath it all she seemed a young and ingenuous creature. She seemed a little girl playing dress-up in her mother's clothes.

"I know!" his mother exclaimed, jolting him out of his reverie. "Your cousin Walter!"

"Walter?"

"Yes. You know, Herbert's son. The male nurse."

"What the devil are you talking about, Mother?"

"We can introduce your secretary to Walter."

Nathan saw red. "No! Absolutely not."

"But why? He's a perfectly nice young man, and he's eligible."

"For one thing, Walter's a bore. The only thing he can talk about is inserting tubes into various orifices of the human body. For another, you have no right. Interfering in my life is one thing, but when you start matching up strangers..."

"I'm not. I hardly expect them to strike up a lifelong relationship. I'm simply providing them temporary company for the day—and time for you to get to know Susan. Wait till you meet her, Nathan. I know you're going to like her."

dredged up for me.''

"Why? Because they're more serious than the ones you usually date?''

"Oh, they're more serious, all right.''

"There's more to beauty than mascara and push-up bras, Nathan.''

"Mother!'' Nathan laughed in spite of himself. "I don't believe you said that!''

A beep sounded. "Oh, I have another call coming through, sweetheart. I'm going to have to run. Thanks for calling, and don't worry, I'll have a room ready for your secretary.''

Nathan hung up the phone and, still smiling, sat back. But as he mentally replayed the conversation he'd just had, he wondered what he'd actually accomplished.

"Nothing,'' he whispered, his smile drooping. He'd gotten nowhere with his mother. This Susan person was still being invited, and he was still expected to meet her and like her and be partnered with her through the weekend—and beyond.

On a surge of self-righteousness he picked up the phone again. "Hello, Mother? Are you still on the line with whoever interrupted us?''

"No. It was only a telemarketing call.''

"Good. I've been thinking about our conversation, and, to put it bluntly, you've got to stop trying to organize my life. I feel really uncomfortable when you bring women to the house for me to meet, and it's got to end. Quite frankly, my social life is nobody's business.''

Apparently, he'd spoken more forcefully than intended. "Well, excuse me for breathing!'' his mother responded.

Nathan closed his eyes and pinched the bridge of his nose. He was tired of this bantering, tired of pretending the game they were playing wasn't rooted in something deep and dark. "Mom, listen. I know you mean well, and I appreciate the effort you're making. But, please…I'm okay."

His mother must've heard the change in his voice, because hers became quieter and more honest, too. "I worry about you, Nathan."

"I know."

"It's been five years already, and, well, you seem to be having trouble…moving on. I just want to help. I want to see you happy."

"I know, and I am happy. Really. I *choose* to remain single. I like my lifestyle. It's not a reactionary thing. It has nothing to do with losing Rachel and Lizzie."

"Are you sure?"

No, he wasn't sure, but he said yes anyway. "And you're wrong in thinking I haven't moved on. Of course I've moved on." Even as he said this, though, memories rose like bubbles through murky water. Pain lanced his heart. "I'm at an entirely different place in my life right now," he continued. "You're just having trouble accepting that place."

"You're right. I'd rather see you settled."

He tried to laugh. "No time. My work keeps me too busy to develop a serious relationship."

"But you seem to have enough time to run off on ski weekends and attend concerts and plays…"

"You're absolutely right. I work hard, but I play hard, too, and that's just the way I like it."

"Forever?"

Nathan chuckled. "Why not?"

"You're only thirty-three, honey."

"Meaning?"

"Seems like quite a lot to me."

"But where's the grounding, Nathan? Where's the per-
manence and the love?" He had no answer, and so she
continued. "You used to be such a happy family man at
one time, such a contented husband. And that little girl of
yours, your life revolved around her."

"Yes, well, that was then." Nathan was feeling decid-
edly uncomfortable now. Pia was cutting too close to the
bone. "Of course, I'll always remember Rachel and Lizzie,
but as you say, a person has to move on. Mom, I really
can't stay on much longer."

Pia sighed. "Okay. I can take a hint."

"Oh, and just a reminder—I'd appreciate it if you'd
avoid references to them this weekend. All that happened
in another lifetime."

"If that's what you want."

"It is." Nathan took a breath and mentally shifted into
a lighter gear. "And that brings us back to the issue that
started us off, my request not to be saddled with this Susan
person."

"I don't know what I can do about that now, dear." Pia
seemed to have shifted gears, as well. "I've already invited
her and can't very well tell her not to come. She knows
I'm planning to introduce you, too. Besides, she's quite
pretty. She's smart and interesting, too. If you object to her,
I don't know what'll please you."

"Letting me find my own women will please me.
Allowing that I'm capable of making decisions for myself
will please me…"

"Well, of course you're capable, and you always do
make your own decisions. I'm merely providing someone
for your consideration. It's entirely your choice whether
you make something of it or not."

Nathan's shoulders relaxed. It *was* his decision, wasn't it?

"Thanks for seeing my side of things, Mother."

"No problem. See you tomorrow night."

Nathan put down the receiver, sat back and smiled. It didn't take more than a moment, however, for him to realize his mother had gotten the upper hand again. "Damn!" he spat, pushing a hand through his already disheveled hair. A matchup was still in the making. He couldn't even use Margaret as an excuse anymore. She was destined for Walter. Nathan felt almost as sorry for her as he did for himself.

There had to be a way out of this, but what? What excuse would stand up to his mother's cast-iron will? What situation would preclude him from being an eligible companion?

He stared at the phone, thought of calling again, but abandoned the idea because he couldn't come up with a ploy. He'd already used the strongest he had, honesty, and that hadn't worked.

He glanced at his watch. It was half-past six. Perhaps he should just call it a day, go home and have a drink. When he was relaxed something might come to him. Sure, a solution was bound to occur. It always did.

Feeling somewhat more sanguine, Nathan slipped on his jacket, turned off the lights and left the office.

At 7:10 on Friday evening, twenty whole minutes before Mr. Forrest was supposed to meet her, Meg was already waiting in her car in the parking lot of Forrest Jewelry— and wondering if she was totally out of her mind.

It had finally occurred to her today just what she was getting into: a weekend spent in the company of people with whom she had absolutely nothing in common. What ever would they talk about? The stock market? Jetting off they wouldn't serve stuff like artichokes or snails. She had no idea how to attack either food. And what about her clothes? Had she packed appropriate outfits?

Meg didn't need these worries about social gaps and faux pas. She had enough anxiety already, worrying over Gracie. She hoped the child wasn't too disappointed over the collapse of their weekend plans. She also prayed nothing calamitous would happen while she was gone.

When Meg wasn't concerned over her daughter, she had Vera and Jay to think about. They didn't like the idea of her working this weekend. Didn't understand it at all, in fact, especially the part about going to Bristol—so much so that they'd almost refused to baby-sit.

But if she had to choose one concern above all others, it was Mr. Forrest—spending so much time with him under such unusual conditions. For one thing he was her boss, and authority figures in general made her nervous. For another, well, there was all that masculine charisma. She could handle it in small doses, but faced with two whole days of it, she was afraid she might do something stupid.

With a groan Meg tried to think of something else. Gazing through the windshield, she realized to her dismay that at 7:15 on a Friday evening in early September, the parking lot of Forrest Jewelry was eerily empty and poorly lit. Not the best of places for a woman to be sitting in her car all alone.

You asked for it, she chided herself. And she had, literally. She'd asked Mr. Forrest if they could leave a little later than planned. That had allowed her time to go home after work and have supper with Gracie. Not that Meg had eaten much. She was so keyed up over the upcoming weekend she'd barely been able to swallow water.

Mr. Forrest had suggested going by her house for her, but, of course, she couldn't allow that. He might discover

Gracie. So she'd convinced him it was no trouble at all for her to return to the factory. None, whatsoever.

She shivered as dry leaves skittered along the pavement and ticked against the door of the car. *Serves you right. You should've told him the truth long ago.*

Suddenly Meg gasped in pain. She jerked her hand away from her mouth and realized she'd been gnawing on her thumbnail. In the thin light of dusk she could see a bead of blood. "Will you relax, Margaret Mary!" she admonished herself as she dug out a tissue from her purse.

Relaxing wasn't in her cards, though, because almost simultaneously a muted gold sports car turned in at the gate. She'd never seen the car before, but she certainly recognized the man behind the wheel.

Moving with breathless urgency, she pulled her keys from the ignition, grabbed her purse, opened the door and in her rush to clamber out of the car, whacked her head on the door frame. Tiny white lights danced a polka in front of her eyes.

That knocked some sense into her, finally. She straightened, took a few deep breaths, and by the time Mr. Forrest was getting out of his car, she felt more composed.

"Good evening," she said, tugging and smoothing her suit jacket. It was the same suit she'd worn to work, and suddenly she wondered if she shouldn't have changed. He had—out of his suit into casual twill pants and a cotton sweater whose pale cream color brought out the depth and attractiveness of his tan. Meg felt fish-belly white in comparison, especially since her suit was powder-blue. Powder-blue tended to wash her out.

"Hi," he said, returning her greeting. "Do you have a bag?"

"Oh, yes." She opened the back door of the Escort and pulled out a battered red valise. When she turned, she no-

...was studying her. He glanced away quickly. Oh, Lord, did she look that bad?

He took her suitcase from her and fitted it into the trunk of his car. His bag was in there too. Not until she saw the two together did she realize just how battered hers was. And, boy, was it red.

Hiking up her skirt, she folded herself into the low-slung car. He slipped behind the wheel, adjusted the volume of a piano concerto drifting from the CD player and eased out of the parking lot.

"The weather's supposed to be great this weekend," he said.

"Yes, I heard." She nested her hands in her lap.

"Temps in the mid-70s..."

"No rain in sight..."

Silence overtook them. *Okay, we've talked about the weather. What now?* she thought.

"This is a very nice car."

A smile graced Mr. Forrest's face. "It's a 1963 Studebaker Avanti, completely reconditioned."

Meg searched for a follow-up but found her mind blank. "I'm sorry, but my knowledge of cars is appalling."

"That's okay. Not many people recognize the Avanti. Suffice it to say, it's a classic. Most design experts hold it on a level with fine art. In fact, when it came out, it was exhibited at the Louvre."

"Oh, my." Oh, my? She never used the phrase *Oh, my.*

"I don't drive it regularly, of course, just on selected trips, such as this one down to my parents' farm."

Meg's thoughts shifted. "That reminds me, before we get there, I want you to know I don't need to be entertained or anything. And I definitely don't want to horn in on what should be a family-and-friends-only affair. In fact, I'd *prefer* to have some time to myself. I've brought along a book

I've been eager to get to. So unless you need me, I don't mind being left to my own devices.''

Mr. Forrest chuckled. "I can see how much you're looking forward to this weekend.''

Her cheeks warmed. She was trying to find a way to deny his statement when he added, "I appreciate this, Margaret. I know how much of a sacrifice you're making.''

Oh, no, you don't, she thought even while she said, "No problem.''

He sighed. "Well, actually there might be.'' Meg wished he didn't sound so serious all of a sudden. "I called my mother last night and found out she's arranged another one of those maddening pair-ups I mentioned to you.''

"Oh, dear. I guess that means you'll need me to be conspicuously present after all, huh?'' Meg had really hoped to be excused from that particular duty.

"It's worse than that.'' Meg heard him swallow uncomfortably and noticed his fingers flexing around the wheel. Good grief, Nathan Forrest was nervous! She hadn't thought it was possible. "My mother's found a way around your presence. She…she intends to fix you up, too. With my cousin Walter.''

Meg swung her head around. "No!''

"Exactly what I told her, but she wouldn't be deterred.'' He dragged a hand down his face. He looked drawn and tired. Odd, she thought, since this seemed sort of a petty problem really.

They drove on for a few miles without speaking. They'd been on the highway heading south for some time. The city had fallen away and the landscape had become more rural.

"So, what are you going to do about it?'' Meg inquired. She did *not* want to be matched up with a stranger.

"I've been asking myself that same question for the past twenty-four hours. I've come up with dozens of scenarios,

...rying from spreading the rumor I have a social disease to claiming I'm gay."

Meg cast him a droll look. "Can't you just reason with your mother?"

He laughed without humor. "My mother doesn't operate on reason." Meg couldn't imagine what sort of woman Mrs. Forrest was, to put her son through such ridiculous torture.

"Anyway," he continued, "the only idea I can come up with that has a fighting chance...actually *you* came up with it, Margaret."

"I did?"

He nodded. "Yesterday. Quite by accident."

Meg frowned as she tried to think back. "I'm sorry. Could you be more spec—" And then it hit her. She finished the word "specific" on a whisper.

"What I'm referring to," he said slowly, reluctantly, keeping his eyes locked on the road, "is your suggestion that we tell people we're a couple, we're dating."

Meg's lips parted, but she couldn't speak. She just sat there, frozen in disbelief.

"That'd work, wouldn't it?" he said uncertainly after a stretch of silence. "If I was already with someone?"

Meg considered his proposal for a while, but ended up shaking her head. "It doesn't have a snowball's chance."

"Why not? My mother will *have* to cease and desist if I'm already spoken for. It'll solve *your* problem too. Or have you forgotten about Walter?"

"But nobody will believe it."

"Why not?"

Meg felt heat coming off her in waves. "I'm not exactly your type."

"Well, no..." Although it was the truth, it still hurt to hear him admit it. "But if I present you as someone I'm seeing, they'll have to accept it. Who'd have the gall to

challenge us?'' Meg noticed his usual confidence was returning. He'd only needed to get over the hump of introducing the awkward subject. Now that he was into it, his
voice was strong and he had an answer for every argument.

''It's pretty desperate, don't you think?''

He shrugged. ''These are desperate times.''

''But someone is bound to notice we hardly know each
other. There'll be gaffes in conversation, questions we can't
answer about each other.''

''No problem. We can say we just recently started dating
and still have a lot to learn.'' He turned a hopeful look on
Meg. ''Well? How about it? Are you game?''

''Wait. No. Who am I supposed to be?''

''Oh, you'd still be one of the office girls. No sense in
trying to be someone you're not.''

''That statement's so absurd I don't know where to begin
laughing.''

Nathan reached across the seat, curled his hand over her
shoulder and gave it a sympathetic squeeze. ''I realize your
job will be harder now. More will be expected of you. So,
naturally, your pay for the weekend will reflect the difference.'' He waited.

She took the bait. ''How much of a difference?''

When he named the sum, she groaned. He was making
this so very difficult.

''Well, Margaret?''

Chewing on her raw thumbnail, Meg weighed the money
she'd be making against the absurdity of the ploy. She
thought about how much she wanted to be living on her
own—and about Gracie, whom this job was all about. For
Gracie Meg could get through anything.

''Sure, I'll give it a shot.''

''Great.'' Nathan Forrest smiled, the corners of his eyes
crinkling more attractively than ought to be allowed. ''In

that case, I suggest you stop calling me Mr. Forrest and start calling me Nathan."

"Likewise, most people call me Meg."

"They do? Why didn't you say something sooner?"

She shrugged. "You seemed comfortable with Margaret."

"Meg," he repeated, nodding receptively. "Yes, that's much better."

It was full night by the time they reached the Forrest home. Still, as they turned in at the gate, there was enough light cast by lamp posts and floodlights for Meg to see it was not the sort of place she'd expected. Of course she'd envisioned something nice, but what faced her was so beyond nice it put her in a holy fright.

At the top of the long tree-lined drive rose a two-and-a-half-story house built of stone and stucco with a multigabled roof line, several tall chimneys, clustered windows and a formal porte cochere. The front lawn resembled a park.

"This is your family's *farm?*" Meg braced one hand on the dashboard, like someone expecting a crash.

"Yes. Beechcroft. It was built in 1906 in the style of a 17th-century English manor house." He cast her an apologetic glance. "I know, it comes across as ostentatious, but after a while you'll see it's really very comfortable."

Meg doubted that.

Nathan brought his car to a stop under the porte cochere and turned off the engine. "Ready, Meg?"

"No, but the sooner we get introductions over with the better, I suppose."

"That's the spirit."

The front door opened before they'd even got their bags out of the car. "Nathan! You finally made it!" A young woman dressed in slim jeans and a hot-pink shirt threw her arms around his neck and gave him a loud smacking kiss on the cheek. She was tall, lithe and attractive. Stepping back, she said, "And this must be Margaret. Hi. I'm Nathan's sister, Tina." She smiled broadly and held out her hand.

Meg would've known she was his sister even without her saying so. She had the same glossy black hair, the same sapphire eyes, the same mouth, although hers was delicate and thoroughly feminine.

"Pleased to meet you, Tina." In her relief at finding someone at Beechcroft who seemed quite down-to-earth, Meg gave Tina's hand several overzealous shakes. Tina's eyes brimmed over with amusement.

"Come in, come in," she said, holding open the massive door for her brother and Meg to pass through.

Stepping inside, Meg tried not to gawk, but yikes! Overhead gleamed a crystal-and-brass chandelier as big as her kitchen stove. The floor was pink-veined marble. Genuine oil paintings in gilded frames graced the walls. Massive bouquets of fresh flowers adorned side tables. And the staircase was wide enough to fit five men abreast.

"Mom told me about your plans to work this weekend," Tina scolded her brother.

"Yes, it can't be helped." Nathan placed the two suitcases at the foot of the stairs. "Where is everyone?"

"Dad's playing billiards with Grandpa. Keith's upstairs freshening up. He just got here, too. And Mother's in the kitchen driving Lucy crazy, of course. I said I'd keep an eye out for you and tell them when you arrived. Why don't you go make yourselves comfortable," she suggested, waving toward a room on the right. "I'll be back in two shakes."

As soon as Tina left, Meg began to feel uneasy again. From the way Mr. Forrest—Nathan—was avoiding her eyes, she guessed he felt the same.

He ushered her into a room he called the family parlor.

"Have a seat, Meg," he said, indicating a Hepplewhite settee. She sat gingerly and he took the spot beside her.

"By the way, are you seeing anyone back home?"

His question puzzled her. "Me? No."

"Oh, good. Not that word of this is likely to get back to Providence, but if it does, I don't want an irate boyfriend suddenly showing up at my door."

"That won't happen. Don't worry."

They sat stiffly, eyes forward, careful not to touch, like a couple courting in a more formal age.

After a long, taut moment, she asked, "What exactly will be expected of me?" Her breath was coming up short.

"Nothing much. Just act the way you normally would with a man you've just started seeing."

It had been so long since she'd seen anyone, she didn't think she remembered how! Inadvertently she emitted a tiny moan.

"I'm sorry about this, Meg," Nathan said. "I'll do everything I can to make it as painless as possible."

"Thank you."

"I also promise that whatever happens, it won't change a thing about our working relationship. As far as I'm concerned it'll remain as professional as it's always been."

"You needn't worry about me being any less professional, either."

"Good. I'm relieved we understand each other."

Just then footsteps sounded in the hall. Nathan reached over, took Meg's hand in his and whispered, "We're on."

CHAPTER THREE

MEG was still trying to cope with the hot and cold flashes created by Nathan's hand surrounding hers when Tina appeared at the door with her mother. Nathan urged her to her feet and, letting go of her hand, guided her forward with a touch to her back. "Mother, I'd like you to meet Marg—Meg Gilbert, my secretary."

"Pleased to meet you, Mrs. Forrest," Meg said, making sure to shake the woman's hand less energetically than she had Tina's.

Pia Forrest was a pretty woman in her late fifties with an outdoorsy wholesomeness that took Meg totally by surprise. Nathan's complaints had led her to expect a matriarchal dragon, not this easy-going middle-ager with silvery blond hair cut in a youthful chin-length bob and a dusting of freckles across her small, pert nose.

If Mrs. Forrest was displeased by Meg's presence, she didn't show it. What she did show was curiosity. So did Tina. Both women wore expressions that announced what they were thinking: Why had Nathan been holding his secretary's hand when they'd walked in, and why was his hand at her waist now?

Edmund and Zachary Forrest, Nathan's father and grandfather respectively, appeared soon after, having lingered a moment over their billiard game. Shaking Edmund's hand, Meg understood where his children got their height and dark good looks. Meeting Zachary, she understood where Edmund got *his*.

"Shall we sit and have a drink?" Mrs. Forrest suggested.

Nathan guided Meg back to the settee, but this time he

draped his arm along the top rail and sat so close their thighs pressed. Meg noticed the other Forrests exchanging dazed glances. No one could be more dazed than she, though. In fact, if she didn't remember to breathe soon, she just might faint.

Edmund returned from the drinks cabinet with a tray laden with a crystal decanter and several delicate cordial glasses. Nathan waited until his father had poured the liqueur and everyone had a glass before saying, "This is as good a time as any to tell you…I wasn't completely honest with you on the phone last night, Mother."

Mrs. Forrest frowned. "What do you mean?"

"Meg and I are not just secretary and boss."

The moment froze. No one breathed. No one blinked. Meg wondered if Nathan was questioning the sanity of this charade, as she was.

Tina was the first to come to life. "You two are dating?"

"That's right." Nathan curled his hand around Meg's shoulder and tugged her closer. Heat climbed up her cheeks clear into her hairline. She didn't want to blush, but he was holding her so tightly, she was positively mashed against his side.

Pia Forrest looked from her son to Meg as if she couldn't believe what she was seeing. "Why in heaven's name didn't you say something, Nathan? Why did you want to keep your friendship a secret?"

Yes, why? Meg wondered, quietly panicking under her frozen smile. She should've known Nathan was used to thinking on his feet.

"Meg and I just started seeing each other and I didn't want anyone embarrassing her with a lot of questions or insinuating remarks."

Zach Forrest chuckled under his breath. "Gee, now who around here would do something like that?"

Pia missed her father-in-law's dig. She was too lost in

her puzzlement. "Then, you really don't have to work this weekend?"

"No, I do. I really do," Nathan said. "Marg—Meg is along to help." His mother was studying him with doubt in her eyes. Meg heard him swallow. "Convenient, isn't it, my dating a secretary?"

"And totally uncharacteristic, I might add. I was under the impression you didn't allow yourself to think of employees in that way."

"What can I say?" Nathan gave Meg's shoulder another squeeze. "Somehow this little lady slipped by my defenses."

Mrs. Forrest's gaze swept over Meg, making her painfully aware of her unremarkable looks, her inexpensive clothes and the enormous acting job that lay ahead of her. "Well, you must be an extraordinary young woman. I can't wait to get to know you."

Meg squirmed, uncomfortable from the ends of her hair to the roots of her toenails.

To their credit, the Forrests kept the questions polite—how long had she worked at Forrest, did she enjoy her job, where did she live. But before long Meg realized she was skating toward thin ice.

"Have you always lived in the city?" Mrs. Forrest asked.

"No, I'm originally from Missouri. A small town outside St. Louis." She felt a reaction course through Nathan. This was obviously news to him.

"Goodness." Mrs. Forrest's eyebrows lifted. "You're awfully far from home. How did you end up here?"

"It's a long story." Could Nathan feel her trembling? "Let's just say I followed someone of the opposite sex."

"Ah. And it didn't work out?"

Meg smiled painfully. "No, it didn't work out."

"And you never thought of returning home?"

...really. I love Providence.'' After a slight hesitation she decided to explain further. ''I don't have anyone back in Missouri anyway. My parents had me fairly late in life. They passed away when I was in high school.''

''Oh, I'm sorry to hear that. But surely you have other relatives...''

Meg shook her head.

''I had a great-aunt. That's who I lived with after my parents died, but she's gone, too.''

''Do you mean to say you have no one?'' Mrs. Forrest looked aghast.

Meg gulped. This was definitely not the time to announce she had a daughter and a pair of in-laws. Fortunately Tina's fiancé, Keith Nelson, came into the room then, and the question was forgotten in another round of introductions.

''Sorry I'm late, folks,'' Keith said, taking a seat on the sofa beside Tina. ''Traffic was brutal.''

''Keith lives in New York,'' Tina explained. ''He comes up on weekends.''

''What do you do in New York, Keith?'' Meg inquired, hoping to keep the conversation moving away from her.

''I'm an architect.''

Tina beamed at her fiancé. He beamed back. It was clear the two were madly in love. Meg envied them.

''The firm Keith works for is going to transfer him to Providence after we're married. Actually he'll be heading up a whole new office.''

''That's great. When's the wedding?''

''October tenth. Columbus Day weekend.''

''Ah. Not too far off, then.''

Mrs. Forrest emitted a sound of distress. ''Don't remind me. There's still so much to arrange!''

To Meg's relief, conversation settled firmly on the wedding, which would be held right there at Beechcroft.

Apparently the house contained a "salon" that could accommodate the gathering of nearly two hundred.

Mrs. Forrest seemed especially involved with the food that would be served. Tina talked about flower arrangements. Keith brought up music. Nathan, who was one of the ushers, asked about tuxes, and Edmund and his father just kept shaking their heads.

"A refill, Meg?" Edmund asked.

"Oh, no thank you."

"Actually," Nathan said, "I was thinking of calling it a night. I know it's early, but this was a work day for me and Meg."

"We understand, son," his father said.

Meg hoped her relief wasn't too obvious. Conversation had been lively, fueled especially by Tina's exuberance. But Meg was definitely ready for retreat.

Nathan got to his feet and held out his hand to her. Tina shot from the sofa at the same time. "I'll go with you and show you your room, Meg."

Nathan looked quizzically at his sister. "That isn't nec—" he began. Tina glared at him. "Well, all right. Thanks. You can help with the bags."

Carrying both suitcases, Nathan followed his sister and Meg up the front stairs. Below them the parlor was quiet. He knew his family was only waiting until they were out of earshot to start talking.

He left his bag in the hall, and they continued up the narrower flight to rooms that originally had been meant for servants.

"I'm sorry you have so many stairs to climb," Tina said, "but all the bedrooms on the second floor are taken, or will be once a few more houseguests arrive tomorrow."

"That's okay," Meg replied. "I'm used to it. I...take the stairs at work a lot."

Nathan wondered about that hesitation. If pursued, would it lead to some other morsel of information he didn't know about her? He hadn't liked being surprised in front of his parents. But then, he'd asked for it, hadn't he?

Learning about her background did clear up a few questions, though—why she dressed as she did, for instance; why she was so serious-minded about her work. Having been raised by elderly people, Meg now made perfect sense.

Tina opened a door and said to Meg, "The room is small, and the bath's down the hall. I hope you don't mind." She stepped in and switched on a bedside lamp.

"Oh, it's lovely," Meg said with such rapture that Nathan took a second look around. It was one of the simpler rooms in the house. Nothing remarkable here that he could see.

Unexpectedly the door closed behind him. He swiveled to find Tina standing before it, hands on her hips and the devil in her smirk. "Okay, what gives, you two?"

His heart stopped. "What do you mean?"

Tina's eyes drilled into him, then into Meg. "You two aren't really dating, are you?" When neither of them moved or uttered a syllable, she added, "It's okay. I won't say anything. Nathan, for heaven's sake, it's me, Tina."

Nathan's shoulders dropped with a sudden release of tension. "Okay, Squirt, you've got us."

Tina chuckled dryly, shaking her head. "Let me guess— to get Mother off your back?"

"You got it." Nathan took a seat at the foot of an upholstered chaise lounge.

Tina glanced from him to Meg. "So, how did this come about? *When* did it come about? And who *are* you, Marg-Meg?" She sat on the bed, her blue eyes sparkling, eager to hear their tale.

It didn't take but a few minutes for Nathan to fill her in

on all the details. He was aware of Meg throughout, standing by the dresser outside the circle of their conversation, looking mortified.

"I'm really sorry, Tina," she murmured when he was through.

"For what? I adore conspiracies. And my mother really can be overbearing sometimes."

Nathan smiled his gratitude. His kid sister could really be thoughtful sometimes.

"And I promise not to breathe a word. Not even to Keith." Rising off the bed, she gave Nathan's hair a ruffle. "You can't get any better loyalty than that now, can you?"

"Thanks." Grinning, he raked his hair back, but it fell over his brow again.

"Well, I'd better leave you two to your plotting."

Nathan walked her to the door. "Tell me honestly, do you think they bought it?"

"Hard to say. I know they were surprised. Tomorrow'll be the real test. We'll just have to wait and see." She opened the door and stepped out to the hall. "Till then. Oh, and I'll just close this door," she added with a mischievous wink. "If anyone asks, I'll tell them you're saying goodnight."

Nathan waited until his sister's footsteps faded before turning to Meg. "How are you doing?" he asked.

"I could be better." Her voice wavered.

He stepped closer, sure that if he touched her cheeks he'd find them scalding. "I'm sorry. This is difficult for you."

She shrugged one shoulder. "I have no right to complain. I agreed to it of my own free will."

"But the idea seemed a lot simpler than the reality, right?"

A delicate muscle in her jaw jumped. "That's usually the way it is with deceptions. So, you said you wanted to get some work done tonight?"

Nan, let's skip it and get an early start tomorrow instead. Can you be ready by seven-thirty?''

"Yes."

"Good. I'll meet you at the foot of the stairs. That way you won't have to go roaming to find me."

"I appreciate that."

"With any luck we'll put in four good hours before people start to show up. After that we'll be expected to join them." He noticed her trying to suppress a shiver. "There really is nothing to worry about. There'll be an informal buffet outdoors, lots of milling and catching up. Some folks might decide to go horseback riding...''

"There are horses?" Her eyes opened wide.

Nathan stifled a smile. "Yes. Do you ride?"

"No. I'm afraid I don't." She looked chagrined.

"That's okay. You don't have to. How about tennis? Do you play?''

Her distress increased. "No."

"Just asking." Nathan patted her reassuringly on the shoulder. "I hope you don't mind, though, if I sneak off and have a game. My cousin Curt and I play whenever we get together, which isn't often these days. I'm really looking forward to it. He and I have a longstanding rivalry going.''

"Oh, no. Please, don't let me interrupt whatever you normally do. As I said, I don't need to be entertained."

"I'm sure you don't. I'm just trying to reassure you this is a casual affair. A giant family picnic, if you will. You might see my grandfather pitching horseshoes, my mother playing croquet, others sitting in the shade playing bridge or just talking. And the kids...''

"There'll be kids?"

"Oh, tons of them. My father always provides a hayride for them and lots of games."

"Sounds wonderful." Meg bit her lower lip, looking about fourteen years old.

"How old *are* you, Meg?" Nathan said before he realized he'd voiced his thoughts.

"Twenty-three."

"Ah." He hid his surprise well. She was just a babe. No wonder she was nervous.

"Why do you ask?"

"Just curious. Anyway," he went on quickly, "all this activity goes on well into the evening. But I want you to be perfectly clear on this—we can leave any time you wish. Just say the word and we're out of there."

"Thanks." She sighed, her face relaxing somewhat.

"Don't thank me. If we leave, I'll put you right back to work."

"Fine by me." She laughed. "Oh, what about your father's birthday? Do you do cake and presents tomorrow?"

"Cake, yes, but no presents. He insists. He gets gifts from the immediate family, of course, but not until brunch on Sunday."

A slight frown tightened her brow. "I hope I brought appropriate clothes." She stooped, opened her suitcase and lifted out a pair of tan trousers. "This is for tomorrow." She laid them on the bed and added a white blouse and tan vest. "Is that okay?"

The outfit was a little stodgy, but Nathan said, "It's perfect."

She seemed inordinately pleased. She smiled, and Nathan was taken unexpectedly by the sweetness of her features. He had to wonder who the jerk was who'd brought her so far from home and then deserted her.

"Well," he said, turning abruptly toward the door, "if there's anything else you need, don't hesitate to give me a shout. My room is at the very end of the hall on the second floor."

Thanks. Good night, Mr. Forrest.''

"Nathan," he said sternly, closing the door on her soft laughter.

Meg stood where she was, listening to Nathan's footfall on the stairs. Finally, when she imagined he was well into his own room, she turned to unpack the rest of her things.

She'd been given such a pretty room. Unlike the more formal rooms below, this one had a country-cottage feel to it. The ceiling slanted to a short wall with two windows tucked into a gable. The wallpaper was white with an all-over pattern of violets and ivy, and on the ornate brass bed lay a white matelasse coverlet with a lavender underskirt. The chaise lounge was upholstered in fabric that matched the wallpaper. She wondered if she'd get any sleep in such a room or just stay up all night looking at everything.

After a trip to the bathroom, she shrugged into her nightgown, turned down the bed, and slipped between sheets as smooth as satin. Her sigh came from her toes. She disliked this job of lying to the Forrest family, but working conditions weren't too hard to take.

If she were truly honest, it was also rather exciting pretending to be Mr. Forrest's latest love interest. She felt as if she'd stepped into a fantasy. Maybe she should stop being so self-conscious and enjoy the fantasy while she could. Come Sunday afternoon, it would all be over.

On that depressing note, Meg removed her glasses, placed them on the nightstand, switched off the lamp and resolved to get some sleep.

A floor below, Nathan tugged off his shirt and tossed it on a chair. He couldn't wait for this weekend to be over. Every instinct he possessed was telling him this deception was a mistake. But there was nothing he could do about it now.

He unbuckled his belt, slipped out of his pants, removed his watch and tossed it on the nightstand. It clinked against

a small framed photograph he insisted be kept there. His
mother no longer displayed photos of Lizzie and Rachel.
She'd put them in the attic, she said, in a special wooden
chest where they'd be preserved but "out of the way."

Nathan picked up the frame and stared at the image it
contained. Rachel with her laughing green eyes and wide
sensual smile. And Lizzie...ah, little Lizzie. Would he ever
forget the feel of that small bundle in his arms?

Nathan no longer felt the same sharp grief that had crip-
pled him right after the accident. He no longer suffered the
dark depressions that had followed. But he still felt all the
love, and he still missed them terribly. Those things, he
was sure, would never change.

His mother wanted him to move on with his life, get
involved with someone new, maybe start another family.
He understood her viewpoint. The trouble was, she thought
he *could* move on. But how could a man marry again when
he'd already loved to the fullest of his capacity? How could
he start a new family when he'd known perfection in his
first?

And of course there was always the dark side—how
could he risk loving again when he knew how shattering it
was to lose the ones you loved?

With a long sigh, Nathan climbed into bed and turned
out the light. On the nightstand the photo remained.

Meg woke early the next morning. She showered and
dressed at a leisurely pace, luxuriating in the peace of having no one but herself to care for. She loved Gracie to
distraction, but it still amazed her how much energy and
time a three-year-old demanded.

As planned, Nathan was waiting for her at the foot of
the stairs. As soon as Meg saw him, her pulse leapt into a
higher rhythm. Again he was dressed in casual clothes, but
on him even khakis and a polo shirt looked spectacular.

They did each other a polite good morning and continued on to the first floor. Breakfast was waiting for them in the study—orange juice, bacon, scrambled eggs and blueberry muffins. A simple breakfast, the housekeeper called it apologetically when she popped in to see if they needed anything else.

This was simple? Meg thought, as she poured cream into her coffee. The napkins were heavy linen, the butter pats were molded into fanciful flower shapes, and the coffee service was heavy silver.

After serving themselves, Meg and Nathan took their plates to a long library table where their computers and other materials were already arranged. Meg felt better just gazing at them. Work. At least she knew what she was about in that arena.

They worked diligently for nearly four hours. During that time no one disturbed them except the housekeeper, who brought in more coffee. Meg was surprised to find working one-on-one with Nathan a thoroughly enjoyable experience. They meshed well, his strengths to her weaknesses and vice versa. Before the end of the morning they were even anticipating each other's thoughts.

A little after noon, Tina strolled in. "You aren't still working, are you?"

Nathan looked up. "Just finishing—for now, at least." He leaned back in his chair, stretching wide and smiling at Meg. "We did well. A couple more hours and we would've been finished."

Meg returned his smile. "I'll try to sneak back sometime this afternoon."

"Oh, no, you won't." Tina hauled Meg out of her chair. "Enough talk about work. Come on. You, too, Nathan. Nearly everyone is here, and they're asking for you. They're all eager to meet Meg, too."

Meg was suddenly reminded of the charade awaiting

them. During the busy morning, she'd managed to forget, but now tension wound its insidious way back into her system. "Are you sure you need me out there, Nathan?"

He glanced at his sister. "Is that Susan person here?"

"Not yet, but she will be."

"Then, yes, I need you desperately, my darling Meg." He took her by the hand and discovered she was trembling. "Deep breaths, Margaret. Deep breaths."

The grounds of Beechcroft were more opulent than Meg had imagined. On the back side of the house, running the length of the ballroom-size salon, was a stone terrace edged with urns spilling over with ivy geraniums. The lawn was velvety green and extended for acres—to the stable and paddocks in one direction; to tennis courts in another. There was a swimming pool with cabanas, a greenhouse, and garden after garden replete with statuary, trellises, walking paths and sitting areas. In the distance the ocean glittered endlessly in the noonday sun.

The number of people also exceeded Meg's expectations. Sixty or seventy at the very least.

"Are all these people relatives?" she asked Nathan, astounded.

"About three-quarters are, yes. The rest are friends."

They made the rounds, Nathan introducing her. Meg amazed herself by chatting with an ease that belied her inner qualms. It was as if she'd become another person.

Well, actually, she had! she thought to her own amusement.

One of the people she met was Curt Forrest, the cousin Nathan had mentioned the previous evening.

"Ah, the tennis-playing Curt," she said, shaking his hand.

"My fame precedes me, I see." Curt smiled warmly.

She decided he must take after his mother's side. Unlike the Forrests, he had hazel eyes and red hair that shone in

...built like polished mahogany. He did have the Forrest mouth, though. He was tall and solid like them, too.

"And I hear you and Nathan are dating?" His curiosity was blatant.

"That's right," Nathan replied and went on quickly. "So, are you ready to get whipped?" He made a swinging motion with his arm.

"I'm not ready for much of anything, Nate. I guess you didn't hear, I'm just coming off a hamstring pull."

Nathan's face fell. "You're kidding."

"Wish I were."

"Hell!" Nathan seemed genuinely upset. "At the risk of sounding arrogant, you're the only person I know who gives me a good game."

"I'll take you on at billiards," Curt offered.

"Not interested."

"Only because I always beat you." Laughing, Curt clapped a hand on Nathan's shoulder. "I'm about ready to grab something to eat. Want to join me?"

"As a matter of fact, Meg and I were just on our way there."

The buffet was served under a blue-and-white striped canopy on the shaded north lawn. Meg was relieved to see that snails and artichokes were omitted from the menu. Still, it was the most sumptuous spread she'd ever seen, served by professional caterers in uniform. Family picnic, my eye!

With plates and drinks in hand, she, Nathan and Curt made their way to a table where Tina and Keith were saving them seats.

Once they'd dug into their meals, Curt's attention returned to Meg. "So, how did my cousin meet such a charming creature as you?" he asked.

She was unaccustomed to such overt flattery and gave

an unladylike bark of laughter. Curt seemed to find it charming.

"Simple. I went to work for him a few months ago."

"You lucky dog," he remarked to Nathan. "And what do you do there, Meg?"

As she described her job, she became increasingly aware that Curt was studying her—her hair, her eyes, her mouth. "And you?" she asked to interrupt his perusal. "What do you do?"

"I'm a buyer for a department store chain based in Brooklyn."

Tina chuckled. "Curt's being humble. His father happens to own the chain."

Did no one here come from an ordinary background? Meg wondered. But of course not. Curt's father was Edmund's brother, one of four, and they were all wealthy. Inherited wealth, she'd learned. The factory she worked at was only a small part of the big picture.

"Come to think of it," Curt added, "in a few weeks I'll be traveling up here to New England again, visiting our Boston store. Maybe we can get together for dinner, the three of us. Or how about that WaterFire I'm hearing so much about? I'd love to see that."

Meg didn't dare look at Nathan or his sister. But through her mind ran the phrase, "What a tangled web we weave..."

"Sure," Nathan said evasively. "Call me when you get into town. I'll see what my schedule's like."

"We can do better than that." Curt pulled an electronic calendar from his shirt pocket. "How about Saturday, three weeks from today?"

With a low growl of irritation, Nathan agreed. Meg imagined he'd call his cousin with an excuse sometime before then.

They'd almost finished their lunch when Pia Forrest approached their table. With her were two women, one about her own age, the other in her late twenties.

The young woman was stunning. Her hair was pale blond and reached her shoulder blades. Her eyes were emerald green. And although she was above average in height she walked with regal bearing. All three men at the table, including the soon-to-be-married Keith, stared at her with embarrassing candor.

"May I interrupt just a moment," Pia said. "I'd like to introduce my friend, Mildred Corning, and her daughter Susan."

Meg's eyes shot to the young woman again. *This* was Susan Corning? *This* was the matchup Nathan was so intent on avoiding?

Mrs. Forrest had introduced everyone at the table before Meg had gathered her wits. Only then did she notice that Tina was staring at her, frowning. Had Tina seen something in her expression? How disheartened she was? How toadish she suddenly felt in comparison?

"Do you mind if I sit with you?" Susan said, already pulling out the only empty chair at the table.

"Be our guest," Tina's fiancé answered.

Once Susan had settled with the group, the two older women moved on.

"Have you eaten yet?" Curt asked her.

"Yes, thanks. I hope I'm not interrupting anything, but I wanted to say hi, especially to you, Nathan." She leaned across Meg and pressed her fingertips to his bare arm. "I know our mothers concocted some plan to introduce us today. But, of course, that was before they realized you were bringing someone." Her forthrightness was disconcerting. It was also damned admirable, Meg thought. It announced her as a woman who spoke her mind and went after what she wanted.

"Yes, it was a classic case of crossed wires," Nathan

returned. Meg almost felt sorry for him. She'd never quite
understood the term "hoisted by one's own petard," but
suddenly she was sure that if Nathan had a petard, he was
being hoisted by it now.

"Maybe some other time," Susan said. The way she kept
her eyes on Nathan, Meg might not even have been present.

"Do you live here in Bristol?" he asked casually—a
good imitation of not really being interested.

"No. Across the bay in Newport. I've just opened a
small shop on Bellevue that specializes in sporting goods
for women."

Susan proved to be not only a beautiful woman but an
interesting one as well. She kept their company for more
than an hour, talking about business, antiques, current news
and sports. It became increasingly evident she knew a lot
about one sport in particular, tennis. When asked why, she
explained that she'd played on a semipro circuit until just
a couple of years ago.

Curt slapped his hand on the table. "There you go, Nate.
There's your tennis match. I bet she'd give you a damn
fine game."

Tina, who was normally very talkative, had settled into
a simmering silence for some time. Now she said, "Nathan
has other obligations today, Curt." Tension suddenly hovered over the table.

"It's okay, Tina," Meg said. "I don't mind. Nathan was
really looking forward to playing today."

"In that case," Susan said in a purring tone, "I'd love
to play you, Nathan. But, Meg, are you sure you can spare
him for that long?"

"No problem." Meg congratulated herself for sounding
so cavalier. "It'll give me a chance to play my own game."

Nathan swung to look at her. "Your game? What's
that?"

Ignoring him, Meg smiled at Curt and replied, "Billiards."

CHAPTER FOUR

NATHAN was just emerging from the pool house, freshly showered after his tennis game and cool-down swim, when Tina caught up with him. "There you are," she said. He didn't like the fire he saw in her eyes.

From the pool, Susan called out a cheery "Hi" and resumed swimming laps.

"How was your match?" Tina asked, crossing her arms.

"She gave me a good workout." Nathan flexed his shoulders. "I feel great. Much looser."

"Well, bully for you."

He sighed. "Okay, what's the matter?"

Tina threw up her hands. "What do you think is the matter?"

He answered irritably, "I—don't—know."

Tina jerked her head toward the pool. "Is she expecting you to stick around admiring her, or what?"

"Yes, but she'll cope." He took Tina's arm and started across the lawn toward the house. "Let me take a wild guess. You think I should've stayed with Meg."

"Give the man a cigar!"

"Well, let me clue you in. *I* think so, too. I wasn't the one who brought up the subject of playing tennis with Susan. I didn't say a word, in fact. Everyone else at the table decided the issue for me, including Meg. Or didn't you notice that?"

Tina cast him a peevish glance. "You still could've made up some excuse if you'd really wanted to get out of it." They walked on a bit further. Finally she conceded. "All right, I'm sorry for getting angry. It's none of my business what you do or who you do it with.'' With a grin, she injected, ''That's Mother's department. I guess I just want to know what the game plan is now, so I'll be able to act accordingly.''

''Game plan?''

''Yeah. Do you intend to dump Meg and spend the rest of the day chasing the Nordic goddess?''

Nathan chuckled. ''You've taken a liking to her, haven't you?''

''To Meg? Yes, I have. She's a very likeable person, or haven't you noticed?''

He gave a negligent shrug. ''That's beside the point— the point being, I'm not interested in Susan Corning. The only game I wanted to play with her was tennis. And, no, of course I don't plan to dump Meg. I fully intend to continue the pretense that we're dating. Mother has to learn she can't keep arranging my life.''

Tina paused, planting her hands on her hips. ''Well, you're going to have to do a more convincing job than you've done so far. Except for some lukewarm hand-holding, you've been the poorest excuse for a suitor I've ever seen. And if you think Mother hasn't noticed, you're dumber than I thought.''

Nathan scowled. ''Mother's been watching?''

''Like a hawk.'' Tina continued walking. ''And you two are the field mice.''

''Damn.'' He gazed toward the house. ''Where is Meg now, do you know?''

''Last time I looked, she was still playing pool.''

''She's really playing? I thought she was just bluffing— you know, to make me think she had something to do.''

''Oh, she wasn't bluffing. She's pretty good, in fact.''

''Against Curt?'' Nathan asked doubtfully.

''Aw, heck, she's already beat Curt four games out of six.''

"You're joking!"

"Nope. Then she took on Keith and Uncle George." Tina shook her head. "Shame on you, Nathan. You should know stuff like that about your sweetie. Maybe you should spend more time with her, hmm?" Her dig was pointed.

They'd reached the terrace. Nathan paused with his foot on the first step, his hands in his pockets. "I don't like to pry into people's lives, especially employees."

"Why? Because they might pry into yours?" Tina sighed in exasperation. "It's called conversation, Nathan. It's called being considerate to someone who's doing you one heck of a favor."

Nathan nodded. "You're right." He felt like a jerk.

"And if you can't do it to be nice, do it for your own survival. Remember Mother."

Nathan laughed, thanked his sister for her advice, then went inside in search of Meg. But when he entered the billiards room only Keith and his uncle George were there, playing each other.

"Do you know where Meg is?" he asked them, growing annoyed. He'd been hoping to watch her play.

Keith chalked his cue stick, his eyes on a difficult shot. "She went off with Curt."

Nathan's stomach clenched. He liked Curt. They were the same age and had always been close. But they did have this fixation with competing. "Do you have any idea where they went?"

"They were talking business."

"Business?" Nathan's voice leapt an octave.

"Mm. Jewelry. Your new line, I think. She told Curt he could take a look at it if he was interested. Does that help?"

Nathan thanked Keith and tried not to leave at a run.

The door to the study was closed, but he could hear voices within. Soft voices. Silky murmurs. Long silences. New line, my foot! he thought as he barged in.

"Oh, hello, Nathan," Meg said with a chipper smile, hands braced on the library table. Nathan stopped in his tracks. If she was being seduced, his cousin had lost his touch.

Curt glanced up. "You've got some good stuff here, pal. Meg's been telling me all about it."

"Has she now?" Nathan exchanged one irritation for another. Meg was a secretary, not a salesman. She didn't have proper knowledge of the merchandise to be speaking with any sort of accuracy to a client.

Curt added, "I hope you don't mind my getting a sneak peek."

Nathan felt perverse enough not to answer. "Could I talk to Meg in private?"

Curt narrowed his eyes, finally sensing Nathan's mood. "Sure," he said, brushing by. "No problem."

"Did I do something wrong?" Meg asked him when they were alone. "Curt said his father's stores've had an account with Forrest for years."

"I prefer that you leave selling to the salesmen, Meg, but that's not what I want to discuss." Nathan led her to the sofa. "I owe you an apology. I shouldn't have stranded you with Curt and gone off to play tennis." His eyes roamed her hair. She was wearing it the same as she always did, but small wisps had come loose and were curling around her flushed face.

"Did you enjoy yourself?" she asked.

He nodded—or thought he did. His attention was fixed on her eyes now. He'd never looked at them so closely before, never realized what a warm shade of coffee they were or how much expression lay in their depths.

"Well, good," she said, smiling.

He forced himself back to the moment. "You're not angry?"

"Why would I be angry? Curt was great company."

"I bet," Nathan grumbled. "He didn't come onto you, did he?"

She laughed. "A little."

"Sorry. I should've warned you about the scope of our competitiveness. But that's getting off the track." He turned to face her more directly, almost taking her hands in his before thinking better of it. "I'm afraid I placed the emphasis of my apology on the wrong syllable. I should've said I was sorry for going off with *Susan*."

"Ah, Susan. Yes, I was a little miffed over that. Hurt, too. I mean, you and I just started dating, Nathan. You should still be too fascinated with me to be looking at other women."

"I know. I'm sorry. I really am." He lowered his gaze.

She leaned in until she caught his eye and then grinned impishly, letting him know she'd been stringing him along. "Of course I'm not offended. This is a pretense, Nathan. Remember?"

Nathan felt momentarily turned around. "Yes, of course. But it still didn't look right—you know, within the pretense. Tina tells me my mother's been watching us and she's not buying the act."

With a sigh of dismay, Meg sat back, folding her hands in her lap. Her brow furrowed. "Want to give it up, just stay here and get some work done?"

Nathan swung to his feet, pulling her with him. "No. Let's go back out there and give it another shot. But promise me you won't be offended if I start acting a bit more...attentive toward you. Do you understand what I mean?"

Behind her dark-rimmed glasses, her coffee-colored eyes grew wide as a fawn's. She swallowed, nodded.

"And you won't misinterpret anything I might do or say?" he added.

She shook her head.

"Good. The last thing I want is my most efficient and promising secretary coming to work with a misunderstanding of what happened this weekend."

Meg met his gaze directly. "As long as *you* don't misunderstand, either, Mr. Forrest."

He nodded solemnly. "Your job is secure."

It seemed a pact had been made, and now that they'd both signed it, they breathed more easily.

The afternoon passed in a dreamlike blur for Meg. That was partially due to the three glasses of champagne she drank. But mostly it sprang just from being with Nathan.

At his insistence, she played him a couple of games of pool. She won one game, he the other. After that he took her to the stable and introduced her to the horses, including his own who was named Foxtrot. From there they joined Tina and Keith on a walk through the gardens and down to the shore. Sitting on the Forrests' private dock, they watched the busy boat traffic on Narragansett Bay, talking all the while about their childhoods, pet peeves, favorite foods, and any other subject that blew their way.

Returning to the party, Meg and Nathan pitched horseshoes with old Zach and then were summoned to another meal. Meg was surprised, and secretly pleased, to discover that Susan Corning had gone home.

"My mother tried to fix her up with Cousin Walter," Tina explained when she and Meg were at the dessert table. "But after five minutes of conversation with him, Susan bolted so fast all I saw was a cloud of dust." The two women laughed companionably.

Throughout the afternoon Nathan made good on his warning to pay more attention to Meg. From the moment they left the study, he barely let her out of his sight. He listened thoughtfully whenever she spoke, laughed at all her corny jokes and made sure she never wanted for anything—food, drink, a comfortable chair.

He touched her constantly, too—a hand to the waist, a brush of a finger along her cheek, a touch of a napkin to her lips. Whispering in her ear became a habit as well, making mundane comments appear to be lovers' secrets. He also learned her full name was Margaret Mary and took to calling her Maggie Mae, a pet name she might have taken umbrage with if anyone else had initiated it. Because it was Nathan, she fell in love with it instead.

By the end of the day, his affectionate treatment almost felt natural to her. That didn't mean she'd grown immune, however. Quite the opposite. Every nerve ending in her body hummed with ultrasensitized awareness of him.

"You're a champ, Meg," he said in an undertone, as they waved off the last few guests heading to their cars. His parents had already gone inside with the relatives who were planning to stay over. "I swear, you could take up a career on the stage."

Standing with her arm around his waist, her thumb tucked into one of his belt loops, she murmured, "Thanks. I'm trying." But the truth was, she wasn't putting all that much effort into it. She'd merely lifted the controls she usually kept in place and allowed her natural instincts to flow. It was easy to seem infatuated, easy to gaze at Nathan with stars in her eyes, because all that behavior was already there within her, ready for the tapping.

"Getting cool," he commented, gazing up at the dusky sky, lit by a silvery three-quarter moon. "Let's go inside." With a hand to her waist he guided her toward the terrace. Light was pouring from the long French windows of the salon as they climbed the steps.

"Your parents have a lovely home, Nathan," she murmured.

"It is nice, isn't it?"

"They're nice, too. Your whole family is. You're a lucky man."

Nathan slipped his hand higher up her back, turning her to face him. His other arm came around her so that she was standing in the circle of his embrace.

"Yes, I am," he answered softly. Then dipping toward her ear, he whispered, "I'm going to kiss you. Okay?"

Meg could no sooner answer him than she could fly. Her heart beat in her throat when she gazed into his eyes and saw how intently they were burning. She hadn't thought he'd go this far in the charade. But, yes, she could see he was definitely going to kiss her, and after spending the entire day in his dazzling company there was little she could do to protect herself or pretend it wasn't exactly what she wanted to have happen.

Slowly he lowered his head and covered her lips with his. Meg sighed against him, wrapping her arms around his neck and giving in to the pleasure swirling through her.

Within seconds, though, he raised his head—jerked it really—a frown in his eyes as he searched her face.

"What?" she whispered, dismay coursing through her.

"Oh, Maggie Mae, where'd you learn to kiss?" he asked. Before she could answer he pulled her close again and with a soft moan resumed kissing.

Meg knew Nathan's parents were in the salon and this kiss was nothing more than a bit of window dressing for their benefit. Still, it didn't feel like window dressing. In fact, it felt incredibly real, from the rapid thudding of his heart to the urgent way his lips were moving over hers.

By the time he lifted his head, every cell in her body had come awake to him. She released a shuddery breath and slid her arms reluctantly from around his neck. Glory be! she thought. If this was how he kissed when he didn't mean it, imagine what he was capable of when he did!

Tucking her under his arm, he continued across the terrace toward the house.

That night Meg had trouble falling asleep. She lay awake watching the filmy curtains at her windows billow and slide in the moonlit breeze, studying the shifting patterns of moonlight and shadow on the walls...and replaying everything she'd experienced that day.

She couldn't remember ever in her life having such a good time. Couldn't remember ever feeling so dizzy or light-headed, either. Too much champagne. Too much conversation and laughter. Too much Nathan Forrest!

He'd walked her to her room tonight, just as he had the previous night. On their way up the stairs they'd talked about meeting for work the next morning and about brunch and departing. Very businesslike. But when they reached her door, the mood shifted—or so she thought.

She saw his intentions in his eyes, felt it in the very air shimmering between them. He was thinking of kissing her again. But for whose benefit? There was no one looking on this time. There was nothing to prove. In the end he didn't kiss her, but she felt he'd struggled to arrive at that decision.

Lying in her room now, Meg wondered if something had happened between them today that neither of them had anticipated. Had fantasy become reality? Or was it just her imagination? Was she making the dreadful mistake of confusing the two? She honestly didn't know. The events of the day slid and shifted, as ungraspable as moonlight and shadow, as inseparable as curtain and breeze.

"Sleep tight, Maggie Mae," he'd whispered to her at her door. With his index finger he'd pushed her glasses firmly in place and playfully brushed the tip of her nose...then not so playfully traced the contour of her lips.

Reality? Fantasy? The only thing Meg knew with certainty was that nothing was certain. Therefore she had better proceed with caution. It was okay to be hopeful, but she couldn't assume anything.

Turning onto her stomach, she burrowed under the pillow and soon drifted off to sleep.

Meg was more tired than she realized. Her alarm rang the next morning, but she turned it off and went right back to sleep. The next thing she knew, someone was tapping her on the shoulder.

"Meg? Wake up. Rise and shine."

Awareness that she'd overslept hit her like a dousing with ice water. She flew out from under the pillow that covered her head and propped herself on one elbow. Her long hair hung in tangles over her sleep-creased face. "Wha'za matter?" she mumbled.

Tina laughed. "Nothing. You just overslept. Nathan got worried and sent me to check on you."

Meg squinted at the blurry figure sitting in the bedside chair. She reached for her glasses. "What time is it?"

"Eight-thirty."

"Oh, God! I never oversleep."

"Relax. It's not the end of the world." Tina's attention shifted abruptly. "Wow, I didn't realize you had such long hair."

Meg shrugged. "It needs to be cut."

Tina didn't disagree, but she did go on about what great condition it was in. "With a trim and a little styling, you'd knock that brother of mine clear off his pins."

Meg swung her feet to the floor, reminding herself to be cautious where Nathan was concerned. "Now why would I want to do that?"

"Gee, I don't know," Tina teased. "Silly me."

Meg was afraid to look her in the eye. She felt exposed.

Tina leaned closer and dropped the levity. "Meg, I saw the look on your face when Susan came to our table yesterday. This isn't a charade with you, is it?"

Meg couldn't bring herself to continue the ruse. Not with Tina. In little more than a day, she'd come to feel like a friend. "Not entirely. Your brother is a handsome man, Tina. A dynamic person. I'd be blind not to notice. Yes, I have a crush on him. But that's all it is, a crush, a mild fascination really, the same sort I have on movie stars."

"My brother isn't a movie star, Meg."

"He might as well be."

Tina's sapphire gaze became penetrating. "You don't have a clue, do you?"

"About what?"

"How attractive and interesting you are."

Tina sounded so sincere, Meg almost believed her for a moment. Almost. "Thanks for the compliment, but I have no illusions." She rose off the bed and slipped on her robe. "And about the crush, I'd really, *really* appreciate it if you'd keep it to yourself. Nathan wouldn't be pleased if he knew."

Tina pushed herself out of the chair and headed for the door. "I still think you're selling yourself short, and I'll tell you someone else who'd agree. My cousin Curt."

"Curt!"

"Oh, yes. And when it comes to women, he's a connoisseur."

Meg laughed and waved Tina out of the room. She'd heard enough nonsense for one morning. "Tell Nathan I'll be down in twenty minutes."

Nathan was already at work when she sprinted into the study. She poured a cup of coffee and joined him. A lot got done in the next two hours—that, in spite of Meg's feeling that her concentration was scattered. Her attention kept wandering to the man beside her. Occasionally, she'd look up and find him watching her, too, task forgotten. Still, by the time they were called to brunch, the job was finished.

Meg was surprised by the shyness that overtook her as

they entered the dining room and resumed the charade of being a couple. Fortunately today's affair was different from yesterday's. It was small, dignified, and her and Nathan's interactions adjusted to reflect the occasion.

Curt and his parents were there, too, along with a few other aunts, uncles and cousins. They made a tableful. And what a table it was, set with fine crystal and white bone china edged in cobalt. Linens, flowers and candles were in various shades of blue, the color scheme playing up the deep blue eyes most of the Forrest men seemed to have.

The food was exquisite as well, although Meg couldn't have said what she ate. She was so lost in the elegance of it all. The climax, of course, came when the housekeeper rolled in a large cake blazing with candles, the second in two days, and everyone sang "Happy Birthday" to Edmund.

Before Meg could blink, the party was over. The entire weekend was over. Nathan's car was packed with their suitcases and office paraphernalia, and everyone was standing outside, bidding them a safe drive back to the city.

"Don't forget," Curt said, "I'll be in Providence in three weeks."

While Nathan exchanged a few last words with him, Meg thanked Mr. and Mrs. Forrest for letting her be part of their special weekend.

"It was our pleasure, dear," Pia said, embracing her warmly. "I'm sorry we didn't get much of a chance to talk. But I hope we'll see you soon."

"That would be nice," Meg said before remembering there wouldn't be a "soon." This was the end of the charade. "Happy birthday again, Mr. Forrest," she said, fighting off the heaviness suddenly weighing on her.

"Thank you," Edmund said, opening the car door for her. Over the Avanti's roof he said to his son. "You be good to this little lady, you hear?"

Standing apart, a grinning Tina caught Meg's eyes and discreetly lifted her thumb.

Nathan drove home in a distracted state.

The weekend charade had been a success. He'd been spared another unwanted matchup, and the catalogue had gotten done, just as he'd hoped. Now all he had to do was wait a few weeks and when his mother phoned, say he and Meg had broken up. He was practically home free.

Only problem was, he wasn't sure he wanted things to play out like that anymore. He'd enjoyed himself this weekend, really enjoyed himself. Meg had been surprisingly good company.

She had a subtle sense of humor he'd never noticed before and was able to discuss the darnedest things, from aphids to Pre-Raphaelite art. Conversely, when she didn't know something, she became an excellent listener, eager to learn. He liked that about her—the kick she got out of learning and experiencing new things, and so much about this weekend had been new to her. Her eyes had sparkled continuously with the wonder of it all. He also admired her sense of independence. She wasn't the clingy sort. She could take care of herself when alone, striking up conversations and billiard games with equal ease.

But the detail foremost on his mind, of course, was how well they'd interacted as man and woman, how right she'd felt tucked under his arm. He'd never thought of her as a woman before—not *that* kind of woman. He didn't have a clue how they were supposed to return to a professional relationship now.

He gave Meg a quick sidelong glance. She seemed distracted, staring fixedly, a small frown marring her brow. She was probably troubled by the same issues bothering him. Neither of them had said more than a dozen words since leaving Beechcroft.

Nathan drove on a few more miles before finally admitting what had been at the back of his thoughts since yesterday. He was considering crossing a line he'd never breached before. While part of him warned that nothing good could come of dating an employee, another part assured him he and Meg could handle it.

She was different from most people. She was remarkably adaptable and understanding. He was betting she'd be able to keep their private lives out of the workplace. Likewise, when they stopped dating, as inevitably they would, she wouldn't bring resentment and recriminations to the job.

Of course, he might just be kidding himself. For all he knew, she might be the kind who, when they split up, would slap him with a sexual harassment suit. But he doubted it.

In any case, it'd probably be best not to say or do anything rash. Best to be cautious and wait a few days, see how they made the transition back to work. If it went well, then he could make a decision. Start slow. Maybe ask her out to dinner next weekend. He smiled a little. Dinner with Meg. That'd be nice.

The city skyline was already in view. Nathan stepped on the gas as if speed would help time move faster.

"Looks like nobody was interested in stealing my car," Meg said when they were entering the parking lot at the factory.

"Luckily," he added, pulling to a stop beside her rusted Escort. "I really didn't like the idea of leaving it here all weekend." He got out and transferred her bag, then waited until she was behind the wheel and buckled in.

"Thanks again, Meg," he said, leaning on the door. "I don't know how to repay you for all the help you gave me."

"A check or money order will do," she quipped.

He smiled. "It'll be on your desk tomorrow when you

come in. And don't forget, you don't have to punch in till after noon."

"Thanks. Well, I'd better be off."

"Yes," he agreed reluctantly, stepping away. She turned the key in the ignition, and the engine growled...and growled. But it wouldn't turn over. She tried again, with the same result. On the fourth try it was obvious something was wrong.

"Oh, great," she muttered.

"Are you out of gas?" he asked, peering at the fuel gauge.

"Nope. I have half a tank."

Nathan sighed. "Okay, let me take a look. Pop the hood."

After examining the engine a while, Nathan slammed the hood shut again. "Any number of things could be wrong, Meg." The car had been badly neglected. "But I think it's the fuel pump."

"Nothing so easy as a low battery, huh?"

"Afraid not. Come on, I'll give you a ride home."

To his surprise, she stiffened. "No, that's okay. I'll call a cab."

"That's silly. I'm here already."

"But it'll take you out of your way."

"I thought you said you lived near Providence College."

"I do. And you live over on the East Side."

He cast her a droll look. "They're only a few miles apart, Meg. Besides, it's Sunday. There's hardly any traffic. Come on," he said more forcefully. "Get in the car."

Eventually he had her and her suitcase reinstalled in the Avanti. But she wasn't happy. She slumped against the door as far away as she could get from him, chewing on a fingernail.

Nathan puzzled over her attitude all the way to her house. The only reason he could see for it was embarrassment.

She was ashamed to be living in this particular neighborhood. It was obviously working-class, mostly three-decker
tenement houses, some duplexes and single-families sprin-
kled among them. Not the best place in the world to live,
but far from the worst.

He pulled the car to the curb, wondering if he should try
to tell her he didn't care where she lived or what background she came from. But he hadn't even turned off the
engine when she opened the door and bolted for her gate.

Nathan swung out of his car. "Hey, wait up. You forgot
your bag." But suddenly a child's voice distracted him.

"Mommy!" called a little girl with bouncing blond
curls, cherry-pink cheeks and the biggest cornflower eyes
Nathan had ever seen. He stopped in his tracks, puzzled—
and then stunned. Because the child running down the walk
was headed straight toward them. And the woman she was
calling Mommy was Meg!

CHAPTER FIVE

MEG'S heart dropped. She'd spent the entire drive from the factory praying that the Gilberts had taken Gracie on an outing somewhere. No such luck. It seemed her hour of reckoning had finally arrived.

"Hi, sweetheart," she said, opening the gate and lifting her daughter into her arms. "Ooh, I missed you."

Immediately Gracie began to chatter about her weekend. Meg tried to appear attentive, but her mind was on the man behind her. Nathan's footsteps had come to an ominous stop. She dreaded turning around, dreaded seeing his reaction, but there was no point in putting it off. Still holding Gracie, for moral support as much as anything else, she turned. It was worse than she'd expected. Nathan seemed beyond astonishment. Into shock.

"What's going on here, Meg?" He spoke with an unfamiliar hollowness to his voice.

"It's a long story, and I'm sure you're eager to get home."

"Not as eager as I am to be enlightened."

She took an unsteady breath. "Nathan, this is my daughter, Gracie. Gracie, this is Mr. Forrest, the man I work for."

"Hi," Gracie chirped, giving him her most winning smile.

Nathan didn't respond. Didn't say hello, didn't so much as nod. He just stared at the child, then returned his gaze to Meg. Displeasure emanated from him like billows of frost from a freezer. Before Meg could utter another word of explanation, however, Vera had joined them.

"Hello, Meg," she said in an overly friendly tone. Her gaze immediately slid to Nathan. "And who's this?"

Meg was sure if her heart dropped any further, it'd be underfoot. "Vera, I'd like you to meet my boss, Mr. Forrest. Nathan, my mother-in-law, Vera Gilbert."

"How do you do," Nathan muttered, his eyes even cooler now.

"My goodness, Meg, you've spoken about your Mr. Forrest, but you never mentioned he was so young or good-looking."

Dead silence followed. Apparently Nathan was still too stunned to respond to a compliment, and Meg recognized it for what it was—a false inference, one approaching accusation.

"How has Gracie been?" she asked.

"All right, for the most part. But yesterday she gave me and Jay a real scare. We took her over to Toy World, and, don't you know, the little imp got lost."

Meg filled with alarm. "Oh, no!"

"Yes. We were frantic, thinking maybe someone had run off with her, but eventually the salespeople tracked her down. Seems she'd taken off all on her own to go look at the tricycles."

"Gracie!" Meg glared at her daughter, still in her arms. Gracie just giggled behind her hand. She seemed wired. Meg could feel it in the jumpiness of her taut body and wondered how many sweets she'd been allowed to eat today.

Placing a hand on Nathan's arm, Vera added, "I do hope you won't ask Meg to work again on the weekend. I love my granddaughter to pieces, but my health isn't what it used to be, and watching her seven days a week is just too much."

Vera had never complained about watching Gracie before—or about her health. In fact, Meg usually had to argue against her frequent offers just to get private time with her daughter. She was hurt. But the pain Meg felt couldn't compare to her embarrassment. She couldn't believe Vera's nerve. How could she say such a thing to Nathan. Why not wait and tell Meg how she felt *after* he was gone, leave it up to her to decline future offers?

Nathan gazed at Vera with a faintly repulsed expression, then said to Meg, "I'll get your suitcase."

"Where's the Escort?" Vera inquired, suddenly realizing her car was missing.

Meg put Gracie back on her feet and flexed her tense shoulders. "I had to leave it in the parking lot at work. It wouldn't start. Mr. Forrest thinks it's the fuel pump."

"Oh, Gawd. The carburetor in Jay's car last week. Now this?"

"Can we talk about it later?" Meg said quietly, wishing Vera would go inside.

Nathan returned with her bag. "Where would you like this?" His lips were tight, his jaw rigid. Meg needed to talk to him in private. She had to explain Gracie and apologize.

"Would you mind very much carrying it up to my apartment for me? I'll take the laptop. It's lighter." Before he could ask what she meant, she explained to Vera, "The project we were working on this weekend took more time than we expected. I still have to put in a couple more hours on it tonight."

Apparently Nathan caught her drift. He held his silence.

"Do you need help carrying anything else?" Vera asked, eager for an excuse to stay glued to them.

"Thanks, Mrs. Gilbert, but we can handle it," Nathan answered in a tone that even Vera had to understand as a dismissal. "I have some lengthy instructions to give Meg, so the less distraction the better. In fact maybe you could keep your granddaughter entertained for a few more minutes?''

Vera cast Meg a resentful look.

"Please. I've put Mr. Forrest out long enough as it is.''

Finally, her mother-in-law acquiesced. Meg led Nathan around to the back of the garage.

The yard was rectangular, thirty by fifty feet perhaps, which was average for this particular neighborhood. Along the back fence stretched a three-foot-wide strip of garden where Meg had planted annuals and a few vegetables. Plastic whirligigs punctuated the strip with vivid color: yellow sunflowers, their petals revolving lazily in the faint breeze; birds of blue and red and green, their wings windmilling like no bird's wings ever windmilled.

A patch of grass defined a place for four resin chairs. The rest was dirt, hard-packed from play. There were no trees. A canvas canopy provided shade for Gracie's sandbox and other outdoor toys. Neighboring houses crowded in on either side.

Trying not to compare this yard with the estate she'd just left, Meg lifted her chin and gestured toward the stairs. "My apartment's this way.''

Nathan set her suitcase down just inside the door, his eyes roaming. The apartment was small, the space divided into a combination kitchen-living room, a bathroom, and a bedroom which Meg shared with Gracie. Quarters were tight but homey, and although toys were everywhere, the place was meticulously clean.

Nathan's inspection took all of five seconds. "Okay, Meg, what's the story?''

Meg laid the laptop on the small kitchen table, wondering where to start. "I'm sorry I didn't tell you about Gracie sooner. I fully intended to, but it was a case of a small problem snowballing until I didn't know how to handle it anymore.''

His right eyebrow rose imperiously. In the space of minutes, he'd become painfully aloof. "I'm afraid I don't understand."

"Sit down." Meg pulled out a chair for him at the table and sat opposite. Then she proceeded to tell him about the difficult time she'd had interviewing for jobs and her decision, finally, to say nothing about Gracie. "I just wanted to get hired. I wanted a chance to prove myself. No one was giving me that chance."

"I find that hard to believe."

"I don't. I understand the problems involved in employing someone with a small child, especially a single parent. Kids get lots of colds, baby-sitters are sometimes unreliable…"

Nathan had gone unusually still. "You're a single parent?"

"Yes. In any case, I hope you understand what happened. As time went on I found it more and more difficult to broach the subject. I thought people at Forrest would think I was devious. You especially. Actually I wouldn't blame you if you did."

"So where is he?"

"What? Who?" Meg frowned, wondering if he'd heard anything she'd said.

"The child's father."

"Oh." She lowered her eyes to the scarred tabletop. "He, um, passed away a couple of years ago."

"He *died?*"

"Yes. In a car accident."

Nathan frowned at her, though she couldn't fathom what thoughts lay behind his expression. The open, affectionate man she'd come to know this weekend had withdrawn into himself, leaving behind a stranger.

"So all this time you've had a child," he murmured.

"Yes."

"Amazing. I never would've guessed it."

"I hope you'll count that in my favor."

Up went the eyebrow again. "Why would I do that?"

"I've tried to keep my home life from interfering with my job performance, and I think I've succeeded pretty well." Meg paused, squeezing her fingers under the table. "I promise to continue working just as hard in the future, too—that is, if I still have a job."

The frown lines between Nathan's eyes deepened. "You think I'm going to fire you over this?"

She swallowed.

"Good Lord, Meg! I have no qualms about Forrest employees having children. In fact, I find employees with kids are often more stable and reliable."

"And my withholding the information?"

"Legally, you're worrying about a nonissue."

"What about…personally?"

"I wish you'd found time to tell me." His tone became slightly caustic when he added, "It was a long weekend. But—" he shrugged and his attitude lightened "—no real harm was done."

Meg sighed in relief. "Thanks. My job at Forrest means a lot to me. I'd hate to have to move on."

"You won't." Nathan got to his feet.

Meg glanced at the laptop. "Is my keeping this overnight going to be a problem?"

"No. Just bring it in with you tomorrow afternoon."

Gracie came pounding up the steps then, barged into the room and leapt into Meg's arms. "Grandma said I could come home now."

She'd left the door open, and, stepping out to the landing, Nathan commented dryly, "Boy, she didn't waste any time, did she?"

Never does, when I have a visitor, Meg thought. "Well,

thanks again for asking me to work this weekend. The extra money will come in handy, and I had a wonderful time.''

Nathan's gaze moved from her to Gracie as if he was still having trouble linking them. He grunted, a sound that could have meant anything, then left without another word.

Gracie wrapped her arms around Meg's neck and laid her head on her shoulder. ''What'sa matter with that man, Mommy?''

Meg frowned. ''Nothing, honey. Why?''

''He was mad at me.''

''No, he wasn't.''

''But he never said hi.''

Meg made up an excuse, something about Nathan just being worried about work, but deep in her heart she suspected Gracie was onto something.

Meg expected her working relationship with Nathan to change. Too much had happened between Friday and Monday for it not to. She just wasn't certain *how* it would change—which part of the weekend he'd choose to remember.

But as Monday wound down and Nathan still hadn't said anything more to her than a polite, distant hello, she had a pretty good idea what it was.

''Good night, Mr. Forrest,'' she called, heading for the elevator.

''Good night.'' He didn't even bother to look up from whatever he was reading. Obviously he was more upset over her not telling him about Gracie than he'd led her to believe. Surely, though, tomorrow would be different.

But it wasn't. Neither was Wednesday or Thursday. He was so cool and aloof, the weekend might never have happened. Actually it was worse. Before the weekend he'd at least treated her cordially. Now he acted as if she was someone he disliked.

His behavior puzzled her. Something about it was definitely out of whack. On Monday, she'd told the other women in the office about Gracie, and none of them had reacted the way he had. Naturally, they'd been surprised. Some had been merely curious, others delighted. But within a couple of days it was over. They'd assimilated the information and moved on. Why couldn't Nathan?

The only excuse she could come up with was that he really, *really* valued honesty and now considered her a liar, someone he'd rather have nothing to do with.

To say that his attitude hurt was an understatement, and on more than one occasion Meg had to duck into the ladies' room to blot her eyes.

On Friday, though, things got infinitely worse.

"Ms. Gilbert, where's the Brayton file I gave you this morning?"

Meg looked up from her computer, startled by his sharp tone. So did everyone else in the business office; he'd spoken to her from clear across the room. "I returned it to your office."

"When?"

"While you were down in assembly."

"Do you think you could be a little more precise?"

Meg felt color climbing up her neck. "Sometime between one-thirty and two."

"And where did you put it?"

"On the file credenza, right where we're supposed to."

"Well, the Brayton file isn't there. I suggest you check the clutter on your desk, and if you don't find it, backtrack every step you've taken today." He glanced at his watch. "I need that file in fifteen minutes." He turned and left her gaping.

"What on earth's got into him?" Meg heard someone mutter. No one answered. The room was deathly quiet, embarrassed for her.

Blanking her co-workers from her thoughts, Meg tried to concentrate. She was sure she'd carried that file into his office. Maybe she hadn't. Maybe she was losing her mind.

She sifted through all the papers on her desk. She searched all the bins, checked all the drawers, even explored the wastebasket. Dusting off her hands, she backtracked her steps to the lunch room, to the copy machine, to the design department, even to the ladies' room, although why she'd carry a file to the ladies' room was beyond her. Everyone else in the business office scoured their desks, as well.

Finally when she'd exhausted every possibility, she tapped on Nathan's door. "Yes," he barked.

She entered the suite with a knot as hard as a golf ball in her stomach. He was talking on the phone, but he deigned to excuse himself from his conversation long enough to glance her way.

"I can't find it, Mr. Forrest. I'm sorry."

"That's all right. I found it." He spoke so casually, Meg's eyes bugged out.

"You found it?" she said incredulously.

"Mm. It was jammed between the credenza and the wall."

Meg's blood pressure skyrocketed. She wanted to ask him why he hadn't told her. Didn't he know she'd been searching high and low—and feeling increasingly nauseous—for the past half hour? Would it have killed him to buzz her and let her know she could stop? But most of all, she wanted him to explain how he could be so casual now? Didn't her feelings count for anything?

She never got the chance. "That's all," he said. "You can go." Then he swiveled his chair and resumed his phone conversation.

Meg closed the door behind her much harder than was prudent. The receptionist jumped. Meg didn't care. The

nerve of the man! All week she'd been making excuses for
him, but no more.

She could see what he was up to. Oh, yes, she could see.
Nathan Forrest was trying to remind her he was the boss,
she was the employee, and never the twain shall meet.

Simmering with anger, she ducked into the ladies' room
yet one more time. No one else was there fortunately, so
she was able to pace and rant aloud. Gradually her anger
abated.

Leaning on the sink, staring at her pale reflection, she
muttered, "You dummy." Hadn't she and Nathan agreed
to return to business-as-usual after the weekend? But had
she believed, deep inside, that would really happen? Not
really. Even after the fiasco of his discovering Gracie, she'd
come into work on Monday secretly believing they might
be on the verge of something—friendship maybe, although
in her heart-of-hearts she'd hoped for more.

How dumb could she be! Nathan had allowed all those
pleasant experiences to happen last weekend only because
they'd suited his purpose. They'd been part of her job.
Once the weekend was over he'd expected her to return to
her side of the employer-employee fence. But had she?
Evidently she'd done a lousy job, because he'd spent the
entire week trying to remind her.

For a brief moment Meg's anger returned. She felt used,
especially when she remembered the more amorous incidents of the weekend. She felt he was making a fool of her
now. But almost simultaneously her throat tightened and
tears scalded her eyes.

"Oh, will you get over it, Margaret Mary!" she re-
proached herself. "It was just a crush. And you did agree
to be professional when you returned. It's time you lived
up to your end of the bargain."

With a resigned sniff, Meg straightened her glasses,

tugged her suit jacket, left the ladies' room and reentered the workplace.

Nathan's phone rang while he was watching the evening news and eating Chinese take-out at the kitchen counter. "Yes?"

"Nathan? It's Tina."

He turned down the sound on the TV. "Hey, kid. How're you doing?"

"Pretty well. Wedding preparations are wearing me down, though."

"What happened?"

"Oh, a snag in our flight to Maui. A bridesmaid who has to be on the other side of the globe the day of the wedding. Other than that, nothing's *happened*. There's just so much to do."

"What is it, four weeks away?"

"Uh-huh. The problem is I've been reading bridal magazines and trying to follow all their advice and keep to their recommended schedules. Those lists are fine to a certain extent, but is it really necessary that I get my teeth professionally whitened in order to be properly married?"

Nathan laughed. "I hope you filed that bit of advice where it belongs."

"Sure did."

"Good. How's Mother and Dad?"

"Oh, they're fine. Actually, they're the reason I'm calling." Something in her tone put Nathan on his guard. "They want to take you and Meg out to dinner next weekend."

His heart stopped. "You're kidding, I hope."

"Uh-uh. Mother should be calling you very soon, in fact. I thought I'd warn you, in case you want to make up some excuse." A smile entered his sister's voice. "Although, from the looks of things last weekend, my bet is on your accepting the invitation."

Holding the phone against his shoulder, Nathan closed the small white cartons of food. His appetite had deserted him. "I hate to disappoint you, but Meg and I have returned to our usual work relationship."

"Oh." Tina's voice sank. "Why? I thought you two got along really well. In fact, you seemed genuinely taken with her."

"I was acting. Remember?"

"Yes, originally. But…"

"No 'buts.' It'd never work, her being an employee."

"I know it's a sticky situation, but surely you could…"

"Nope. Besides, Meg and I are totally unsuited."

"What are you talking about? She's a lovely person."

Nathan paced as far as the phone cord would allow. "Yeah, well, you only saw one side of her. She was acting, too, and on more fronts than one."

"I…doubt that. She was so open and ingenuous."

"Really? And did that open, ingenuous person tell you she has a daughter at home?" When Tina failed to answer and the silence stretched out, Nathan said, "I thought not."

"Aw, Nathan! She's married?"

"No."

"Oh." Tina's hope rebounded. "Divorced?"

"No."

"She had a child out of wedlock? *Meg?*"

"No!" Nathan said impatiently. "Her husband died."

The line hummed with silence again. *Please let it lie,* he prayed.

But Tina didn't oblige. "The ironies are so thick I'm choking on them," she said. "Did you get to see the little girl?"

"Briefly."

"What's her name?"

"I'm not sure."

"What's she like?"

"I don't know. She's a child. She's...small."

"Aah! That's it, isn't it? You're not asking Meg out because of her daughter."

Nathan thought of denying it, but he was tired of relatives badgering him, tired of having to be defensive. "You're right. I'm not interested in kids anymore. I had one already, and her death left me with scars. I don't know why people have such a problem with that. Why do you think that is, Tina? Why are people so unwilling to leave me alone with my scars?"

He'd meant to put her off. He'd meant to offend. And from the thinness of her voice when she spoke, it seemed he'd succeeded. "Sorry, Nathan. I guess no one really can understand what you went through, except maybe another parent who's lost a child. All I know is I wish I could help. It really hurts to see you stuck in this rut."

Nathan didn't respond. If he remained silent, maybe Tina would let it go.

"Does Meg know about Rachel and Lizzie?"

"No."

"Don't you think she deserves an explanation?"

"No."

"But she must find your behavior awfully strange."

"I don't see why. She understood as clearly as I did that we'd return to a professional relationship when we got back."

"Ah, Nathan." Tina sighed. He could imagine her shaking her head, lips pressed tight. But whatever was on her mind got left unspoken. "All right, I'll drop it for now. I just wanted to warn you about Mom's intentions."

"Thanks. And I'm sorry I snapped at you."

"It's okay. By the way, would you mind if *I* called Meg and made a date for lunch?"

"Why would you want to do that?" he asked suspiciously.

His sister laughed. "I just like her, Nathan. We got along well last weekend. I'm not plotting against you. As I've said many, many times, that's Mother's bailiwick."

Nathan's frown softened. "You'll ask her to lunch anyway, whether I like it or not. I do have a favor, though. Don't tell her about my past."

"Of course I won't. That's your job, Nathan. Yours alone."

Nathan hung up the phone, put the small cartons of food in the refrigerator and, still irked by his sister's parting shot, carried his wine into the living room. He didn't owe Meg anything, certainly not an explanation. His past was no one's business.

But as he settled onto the sofa with the newspaper, guilt fell over him like a prickly mantle. Tina was right. Meg *was* confused and hurt by his sudden retreat. She was angry, too, and rightly so. He'd been acting like a jackass. The least he could do was apologize.

Nathan glanced at the phone. It was Friday night, five to seven. She might be home. Should he call? Would she listen? Or would she tell him to go take a flying leap?

He was still trying to decide what to do when the phone jangled. "Yes?" he answered.

"Nathan, love. It's Mom."

Nathan mentally groaned. He hadn't given an excuse a moment's thought.

Meg cashed her paycheck right after work so that when she got home she was able to give Vera the rent money for the month. It felt wonderful to be paying her own way, finally. These past four months, her sense of self-worth had flourished.

Now, racing Gracie up the stairs, Meg felt energized,

almost euphoric—even if the week had been distressing, thanks to Nathan Forrest. She felt especially good because, working the weekend, she'd earned the equivalent of two weeks' pay. She'd finally been able to make a deposit in the savings account she'd opened six weeks ago. She'd also put aside some mad money for an outing with her daughter.

Meg quickly prepared a supper of tacos, one of her and Gracie's favorite meals, then gathered up the laundry and took it over to the Gilberts' basement to wash. Returning, she packed Gracie into the car and went off to do the week's grocery shopping. Her happy energy stayed with her throughout, even after she returned home and, with Gracie's help, was unloading the bags. She felt light, liberated, optimistic, on her way to better things.

She was unwrapping a frozen juice bar, Gracie's reward for being such a help, when Vera tapped on her door and strolled in.

"Here's your laundry, all folded and ready to put away."

Irrationally, some of Meg's lightheartedness fled. "Vera, you didn't have to do that."

"It was no bother. What're a few towels?" She placed the basket on the sofa. "I happened to notice your underwear's gotten pretty thin, though. I'll make a note to buy a few new pairs the next time I'm at the mall."

Meg's smile wilted. "No, please don't. I can get by for now."

"It's no bother."

"Sure it is. I was thinking of going shopping for myself soon anyway. There are some other personal items I need."

"Make a list. I'll get everything at the same time."

Meg swallowed, feeling increasingly as if she were butting against a brick wall—which was stupid. The woman was only trying to help.

"Thanks, but I'm thinking of changing the style I usually wear."

"Oh." Vera looked crestfallen. "To what?"

"I don't know. Just…something different."

"Don't you like the cotton briefs I've gotten you in the past?" She looked personally offended now.

"Yes, I do. But I thought just for a change…there are so many styles, so many colors besides white…" Meg couldn't believe she was standing here defending her right to buy her own underwear. Before she said something rash, she'd better change the topic.

"Vera, I've been meaning to ask you…you know about credit cards, which charge the best rates and all that. Right?"

Vera pulled out a chair at the kitchen table. "Why do you ask? Are you thinking of getting one?" Her eyes flicked to the counter, right to the three applications Meg had laid out for comparison.

"Yes, I am. Now that I've been working a while, I'm getting lots of offers."

Vera shook her head, then her two hands joined the motion. "Don't do it, honey. Credit cards only get you into trouble."

Folding her arms, Meg leaned against the counter. "But they're so convenient."

"Sure. Too convenient. Before you know it, you're up to your eyeballs in debt."

"You have a few cards, I noticed. Are you in debt?" Unwittingly, an edge sharpened Meg's words.

"Well, no, but…"

"Then I'll just have to use the same restraint." Pushing away from the counter, she said, "Excuse me," as much to end the disheartening exchange as to go check on Gracie, who was playing in the bedroom.

When Meg returned, Vera was poring over the supermarket ads in the newspaper, apparently in no hurry to go home. "Did you buy any of the center-cut pork chops that are on sale this week?"

Meg realized she was feeling tired all of a sudden and wondered where her buoyant mood had gone. "Uh, no."

"You should have. The sale ends tomorrow." She turned a page. "That's what I plan to make for Sunday dinner. Pork chops."

Meg grew uneasy. "Vera, I'm not sure I'll be here for dinner this Sunday."

"Why not?"

Must we always eat together? she wanted to protest.

"I'm thinking of taking Gracie up to New Hampshire. There are so many attractions for kids up in the White Mountains area—if I can use the car, that is."

"You know I never need it on weekends. But, Meg, the expense."

"I have a little extra money because of working last weekend."

Vera's round face puckered. "That's a long drive. At least three or four hours each way."

"I know." Lord, was she tired. She dropped into a chair and sighed. "I was thinking of finding a motel and staying over tomorrow night. That'd give me and Gracie two whole days to explore."

The puckers on Vera's face deepened. "Would you like me and Jay to go along with you? For safety's sake, you know? We could share expenses and help with Gracie, too."

Meg fidgeted with the salt and pepper shakers, turning them, clicking them together. How to tell this woman her company would not be the favor she thought it was. "Thanks, but we'll be fine."

"I don't know," Vera said warningly, shaking her head.

"Of course we will be."

Vera continued to look doubtful. Her eyes never left

Meg's face, assessing, delving for reasons for this hurtful, ungrateful gesture. Suddenly her nostrils flared as if she'd sniffed out an answer. "Are you planning to meet up with that Nathan Forrest again?"

Meg fell back against the wooden chair as if she'd been flung. "Of course not!"

Vera tilted her head. "Are you sure?"

Meg was on the edge of losing her patience. "Vera, I don't know what you think went on last weekend, but, believe me, it was nothing that would lead to my meeting Mr. Forrest again. So, please, no more insinuations, okay?" Meg pushed to her feet, removed a package of hamburger from the fridge and tore it open. She'd channel her frustration into doing something useful.

"Good, I'm relieved to hear it, because I can't think of anything more disastrous than you hooking up with somebody like that."

Meg placed a clean plate on the counter, gouged out a fistful of ground meat from the three-pound lump and pressed it forcefully between her hands. "What do you mean, somebody like that?"

"Well, you know. He's your boss. Plus he's a terribly handsome man."

Meg took up another handful of meat, pressing it so hard it oozed between her fingers. "Meaning what?"

"He can't possibly have good intentions, Meg."

Meg slapped the malformed patty on the plate, knowing full well what Vera was implying. A man like that couldn't possibly be interested in her. The worst part was, Meg knew Vera was right.

Suddenly Meg felt utterly drained. Her hands fell limply to the counter and her eyes began to sting. "I just want to get away," she said in a voice that trembled halfway between anger and pain. "Why can't you understand? I just want to do something different with my daughter, alone."

Vera sat frozen for a moment, then she lowered her eyes and her cheeks drooped. Everything about her seemed to droop, actually. She looked as if she were melting.

"Sorry, Vera, but sometimes I feel as if I can't breathe around here!" It took a moment for her to regain her composure. "Besides, what if I *did* want to go away with a man? Isn't that my business? Aren't I allowed a life?"

Tears glistened in her mother-in-law's eyes. Her lower lip trembled. "I only meant to look out for you, Meg. You and Gracie mean the world to me. If anything bad happened to you, I…I don't know what I'd do."

Meg pressed her lips together and nodded, torn between guilt and self-preservation. Vera *did* mean well, but Meg also knew she could crumble into tears at the drop of a hat. "I know, and I'm sorry I got upset. But you really have to stop hovering and doing for us. You have your own chores, your own life to tend to."

Vera wiped the moisture from her eyes. "Maybe you're right. Maybe I should just go home where I belong."

"Oh, God. I didn't mean…"

"No, no." Vera waved a hand, cutting her off. "I've got things to do."

Grunting, she pushed herself to her feet and started for the door. But then she paused. "Oh, I almost forgot." She reached into her pocket and pulled out a business envelope. "We got the bill for the repairs on the Escort. Now that you're working and insisting on taking responsibility for your expenses, I thought you'd want to handle this, too."

Meg stared at the envelope, feeling she'd just been sucker-punched. She took it from Vera, slipped out the bill and unfolded it. When she read the bottom line, her heart dropped. So much for making progress, for being on her way to better things. She might have taken one step forward today, cashing her paycheck, but as of now she was two steps back.

Vera opened the door. "Well, if I don't see you before you leave tomorrow, have a nice trip."

Meg was still staring at the bill, the print swimming out of focus, when Vera stepped out onto the landing and jumped. "Oh! You startled me."

Puzzled, Meg looked up, leaned out the door and realized someone was halfway up the stairs. Nathan Forrest!

Vera turned, shooting her a look full of renewed suspicion, a look that said, So nothing happened last weekend, eh?

Ah, yes, the dance was becoming familiar indeed. One step forward. Two steps back.

CHAPTER SIX

NATHAN stared up at the two women who, in turn, were staring down at him. He felt like a burglar who'd been caught climbing in a rear window. In truth, he'd only been caught eavesdropping. Somehow, though, his offense seemed worse.

"Mr. Forrest! What are you doing here?" Meg asked.

Good question. Why *had* he come here? Nathan rubbed his jaw. Ah, yes. He'd thought she deserved an apology face-to-face. He'd wanted to reassure her that his boorishness this week wasn't due to anything she'd done.

He grimaced. There was also the matter of a phone call he'd received from his mother a little while ago.

But after the conversation he'd just overheard through the open window, his intentions seemed unimportant. There was something wrong in Meg's life. Very wrong.

Instead of answering Meg's question, he merely said, "Good evening, Meg. Mrs. Gilbert." Hoping he looked confidently nonchalant, he resumed climbing the stairs. "Mrs. Gilbert, will you excuse us, please? I need to speak to Meg about…about her job." It was the only thing his wretched mind could cough up.

The woman's little piggy eyes narrowed, nearly disappearing in her big piggy face. "What about her job?"

Nathan smiled and winked, relying on his much overrated charm. "Sorry. It's top secret." Then, dropping the levity and leaning in, he added, "It really is important, ma'am."

With a hand-flutter to her throat, she stepped aside, letting him squeeze by.

Nathan ushered Meg into her apartment and closed the door. "That woman needs a life!"

Meg seemed surprised by his remark, but she didn't comment. "What's this visit really about?" she asked.

He'd expected her to be angry. She'd been angry when she left his office this afternoon, and that on top of a week of being confused and hurt. But right now Meg didn't look capable of swatting at a fly. Her face was drawn, her breathing tremulous. His dislike of Vera Gilbert deepened immeasurably.

"Originally I came over to apologize to you for being such a jerk all week, but I can see I came at a bad time. You've obviously got other things on your mind. I really should've called first. Sorry. I can leave."

Meg raised a hand to halt his defensive babble. "Give me a minute. I just need to switch gears. And don't you dare leave. I want to hear that apology. I want to hear every last word, especially the part about you being a jerk." Her smile was faint, but it gladdened his heart. "I just need a minute to myself. Okay?"

"Of course."

Meg went off to the bathroom and closed the door, but before she did she dropped something on the kitchen counter. Nathan took a quiet sidestep to bring it into reading distance. It was an invoice from a Williams' Auto Repair. The bill was in the amount of two hundred and seventy dollars.

"Hi!"

Nathan jumped, spun around, and found Meg's daughter smiling up at him. She was dressed in a pink ballerina tutu, with a long strand of plastic beads hanging from her neck. He'd forgotten about Gracie.

"What are you doing?" she asked, brushing aside a long blond ringlet from her forehead.

"Just waiting for your mother. She went to the bathroom."

"Oh." She nodded sagely. "Would you like something to drink? We have milk."

"Uh...no, thanks." He folded his arms, averted his eyes.

"We have orange juice, too."

"No, I'm fine." Nathan reached for a newspaper on the table, uncomfortable with a toddler offering him hospitality. Why was Meg taking so long?

"You can come sit in the living room. That's where my mommy always reads the paper."

Nathan had to agree the child's suggestion made sense. He crossed to the living room area, removed a basket of laundry from a saggy sofa and sat down.

Wrong choice. Gracie landed on the cushion right beside him. "Wanna see my fish?"

He intended to say no, but there was such innocent eagerness in her big blue eyes, he ended up acquiescing.

Gracie took him by the hand, tugged him over to a twenty-gallon tank, turned on the light within the hood and chirped, "Hey, wake up, guys." In spite of himself, Nathan chuckled.

"Oh, I see you have an angel fish."

"Uh-huh. That's Buzz."

"Buzz? They have names?"

"Uh-huh. And that's Woody, and there's Ariel and Pocahontas." She went on, naming all eleven creatures. Then she explained the function of the filter and the thermometer.

"Wanna see my tent?" she said, tugging on his hand again.

Just then the bathroom door opened and Meg stepped out. She inhaled, let out a gusty sigh and smiled. "Much better."

Nathan glanced down at the child, still holding his hand.

His discomfort must have manifested itself somehow, because Meg came to his rescue.

"Okay, Gracie. Time to go put on your pajamas. We'll skip your bath tonight." The child tried her luck with a whine, but Meg stood firm. "Go on," she said. Surrendering to the inevitable, Gracie shuffled off.

"She already dresses by herself?"

"Yes." Meg seemed to take the feat for granted.

"She's awfully bright, Meg."

"Mm. I know."

"Her vocabulary and sentence structure are amazing. She actually used the word *actually* in talking to me."

"Oh, she's been using that since she was two."

"Two!"

"Mm. But she still misuses and mispronounces lots of things. She's just three, after all." A smile softened Meg's face. "My favorite is, instead of Humpty Dumpty, she says Humpy Dumpy."

Nathan laughed. "Does she go to nursery school?"

Meg looked aside, twining her fingers tightly. "No. I was hoping to enroll her this fall, but something happened to her application."

"Oh, that's too bad." He frowned, puzzled.

"Yes. She's certainly ready for preschool, and she's so eager."

"What happened to the application?"

Meg was twisting her fingers so hard he was afraid she'd do them damage. "The school never got it."

"How come?"

"Who knows?" She shrugged. "So? What about that apology you owe me?"

Nathan gestured toward the sofa, but she shook her head.

"Make yourself comfortable, but if you don't mind, I have a chore to clean up here." She went to the kitchen counter where a mound of ground beef and a plate of patties awaited.

He came to stand beside her, leaning his hip against the counter. "I don't know where to begin, Meg. I've been acting so inappropriately toward you—cool, standoffish, rude—especially considering how you went out of your way to help me last weekend. But today's incident with the missing file..."

Meg's hands stilled and her brow became pensive. He wanted to touch her, wanted to stroke her hair, brush the back of his hand over her warm, smooth cheek. But that wasn't why he'd come here.

"That went beyond rude," he continued. "All I can say is I'm sorry. You did nothing wrong. The problem was... was entirely mine."

"I don't understand," she said, slightly peevish. "It certainly seemed like my problem." She was clearly waiting for an explanation. A knot of tension began to tighten in Nathan's stomach. What was he going to do? Not only was his behavior too difficult to explain, he didn't *want* to explain it, either.

Fortunately, Gracie chose that moment to burst from the bedroom. "Got my pj's on."

"Okay," Meg called. "I'll have your milk ready in a sec." Moving quickly, she covered the meat in plastic wrap and placed it in the freezer.

Nathan's attention remained with Gracie. She was playing with the TV equipment, pressing buttons here, turning knobs there. "Uh, Meg..." he said in a low, cautionary voice. But a second later the screen lit up, and then a video started, something called "Little Bear."

"It's okay," Meg responded, misunderstanding his concern. "I usually let her watch some TV before bed. It helps her wind down."

She turned on the faucet and began washing her hands. "So, continue."

Nathan picked up a sponge and wiped down the counter. "Am I forgiven?"

"Depends." A teasing light entered Meg's coffee-brown eyes. "Is your attitude at work going to change?"

"Absolutely. I'll be a model of civility." He placed the sponge on the sink edge and dried his hands on the same towel Meg was using.

"Then, sure, you're forgiven. If you want to know the truth, your apology was unnecessary." Her smile faded. "Today I realized I wasn't acting as professionally as I promised. I returned from the weekend with inappropriate expectations. You had every right to remind me our relationship was a business one."

"Is that what you thought my aloofness was all about, putting you in your place? Good Lord, Meg." He thrust his hand through his hair.

"Well?" she asked.

"I'd like to explain but..." But what? "Later. Now there are too many distractions."

"Okay," she replied uncertainly.

He breathed more easily, resting back against the counter again. "So what were those expectations you had?"

She took down a Snoopy mug from the cupboard. "Friendship. I thought, after all the talking we did, after working so well together..."

"And all the meals we shared, and playing billiards and horseshoes, and duping my mother..." Nathan nodded. "You had every right to expect more of me, Meg." She started to protest, but he held up his hand. "Of course we're friends. But you'll have to have patience," he said, surprising even himself with his candor. "This is new territory for me. I'm making up the rules as I go along."

Their eyes met, questioning, probing, and finally smiling.

"You've got it," she murmured, nodding, then went to the refrigerator for the milk.

Nathan stepped away from the counter, wandered to the door and looked out. "You really surprise me, Meg. I expected you to come at me hammer and tongs." He turned.

"I wanted to," she confessed. "When I went into the bathroom, I tried to get back my anger." She filled the mug with milk and placed it in the microwave. "I tried remembering all the hurtful incidents of the past week. But—" she shrugged "—you caught me at a low point. A lot of other stuff's been going on around here. If you want anger, you'll just have to come back tomorrow."

He smiled. "Tomorrow you'll be in New Hampshire."

She stiffened. "You heard that much, huh?"

"Yup."

She winced. "And the part about my meeting up with you?"

"That, too."

"Great." A wash of pink rushed into her cheeks.

"There's nothing to be embarrassed about, Meg. It was your mother-in-law who was out of line, not you."

Meg removed the warm milk from the microwave and took it over to her daughter. When she returned, Nathan pulled out a chair for her at the table and took the one opposite.

"You said a lot's been going on. Tell me about it. What was that conversation with your mother-in-law all about?" Nathan could see her trying to retreat from the question but he probed again. "I heard you say something to her, something about…not being able to breathe?"

She covered her eyes with one delicate hand and shook her head. "How melodramatic that must've sounded."

"No. It sounded very real, full of very real frustration."

She shook her head again. "I wish I hadn't said it. Vera and Jay have been very good to me. They've treated me like a daughter.'' She went on to explain how they'd insisted she remain living over the garage after their son died, how they'd taken her under their wing, supported her financially and baby-sat for Gracie, free.

''I see,'' Nathan murmured during a pause in her litany of praise. ''So if you complain, you'll come across as ungrateful, is that it?''

''That *would* be ungrateful of me. Terribly.''

''But lots of things about living here bother you. Right?''

She swallowed and said nothing.

''Okay, let me tell you how it appears, then. Stop me at any time if I stray off the mark.'' Nathan sat forward, resting his forearms on the table. ''It appears you've got yourself a pair of in-laws who may be loving and generous, but who are also in every nook and cranny of your life. From the little I've observed, you don't seem to have much privacy. Am I on the right track?''

Meg lowered her eyes but allowed a faint nod.

''It also appears you don't have much latitude to do things on your own.''

Again he sensed her agreement.

''How are they reacting to your working?''

She didn't answer.

''Have they discouraged you from making new friends? Stopped you from dating? Wait. You don't have to answer that. I already know the answer just from Vera's reaction to me.''

Meg gazed at him beseechingly. ''You have to understand they lost their son, Nathan, their only child.''

He nodded, indeed understanding. ''And you and Gracie are their link to him, their way of keeping him alive.'' He watched her eyes darken with desperation. ''That's an unfair burden, Meg. You can't be their son's widow forever.''

''Yes, I've sometimes thought that, too,'' Meg admitted, but immediately looked guilty.

"Please, Meg. You don't have to hold back. Not with me."

Suddenly her eyes grew luminous with tears. "I loved Derek," she said. "And when he died I wanted to die, too. If it wasn't for Gracie…" She lowered her eyes and let the rest of her sentence trail off. "I grieved a long time, but eventually there came a day when it ended. I'll never forget my husband, but I want to move forward with my life." Nathan could see she was making a tremendous effort to contain her emotions, but a tear slipped down her cheek anyway.

"And they won't let you?"

She sniffed and shook her head, but immediately qualified the gesture with, "Maybe it's just my imagination."

He doubted it.

She looked down at her hands, folded in her lap. "If it was just me, I wouldn't care so much. But Gracie's involved. She's the one they're really afraid to lose. As a result, sometimes they do things I wish they wouldn't."

"Like?"

"Oh, giving her too many toys and sweets, for instance."

"On the notion that giving her those things will make them look good in her eyes, win them her love?" Nathan asked. Meg averted her gaze and nodded. He imagined she also came out the bad cop in those instances since she disapproved.

On a hunch, he asked, "Did they have anything to do with the preschool problem?"

Meg swallowed. "I'm fairly certain Vera didn't mail the application."

Nathan arched one eyebrow in silent criticism, but she countered with, "Her intentions were good. She really believed Gracie was too young and would be better off at home with her. She thought she'd be saving me money, too.''

''But she had no right to deliberately upset your plans. That's meddling in the worst sense. It's manipulating.''

Meg's expression seemed to say he didn't know the half of it.

''Meg, for heaven's sake, why don't you just move out?''

''I intend to. That's why I'm working, why I gave up last weekend with Gracie and agreed to go to your parents'. I'm trying to put aside the money.''

''I'm not sure I understand. Why do you have to wait?''

She looked at him as if he had three heads. ''There's a little matter of a security deposit and first and last months' rent. Plus, I'm starting from scratch. I don't own a thing, not one dish, not one stick of furniture. All this belongs to the Gilberts. Even the car I drive is Vera's. If I were alone, sure, I'd make do with a tiny furnished apartment and the bus system. But Gracie complicates things. I won't have her suffering.''

Nathan rubbed a hand over his mouth, seeing her predicament somewhat more clearly. ''But surely your husband left you something?''

She shook her head. ''We got married right after Derek graduated from college. His parents fixed this apartment up for us. They had it all furnished when we moved in.''

''But with an education he must've earned a halfway decent living.''

''He did. But he also had a college loan to pay off. The only thing of value we owned was our car, and he wrecked that in the accident that killed him.''

''Life insurance?''

''Yes, he did have insurance, but it was an old policy, one that his parents had bought when he was a child. They were still listed as beneficiaries.''

Nathan felt a roiling in his stomach. "Why didn't they give it to you? You were his widow. Then you could've paid your own bills or moved into your own apartment."

Meg shook her head. "It wasn't a huge amount. What would I have done once it was gone? The way things worked out I'm sure I got the better end of the deal. I didn't have to go out to work. I was able to stay home with Gracie for those crucial first three years of her life, an opportunity I consider without price."

"In the meantime, though, they kept you on a short leash."

"It was a small price to pay for those years with Gracie."

Nathan leaned on the table, staring at her. "Tell me, if you had the choice, would you be working now, or would you still be at home with her?"

She thought for a moment. "I do enjoy working. I feel good about myself when I've put in a productive day. But in a perfect world, I'd only do it part-time. Very part-time. I think Gracie misses the attention I gave her when I was home." She gazed across the room at her daughter. The look of melancholy in her eyes deepened.

"And I'm sure the attention you've given her is the reason she's so bright and well adjusted."

Meg chuckled. "She was just born bright, but thanks, I don't mind taking a little credit." She glanced at the clock over the stove. "Right now, though, I really have to get her to bed. I've let her watch more 'Little Bear' than she normally sees in a week!" She rose, took a step away, paused. "This may take a while. We have a certain bedtime routine…"

Nathan realized it was time for him to leave, but he felt there was so much yet to say. "That's okay. I'll wait."

"Are you sure? It may be as long as half an hour."

He nodded firmly. "I'll be here."

Meg shrugged and started to walk off, but paused yet again. "Oh, by the way, I've changed my mind about New Hampshire. Tomorrow—" she swallowed with difficulty "—I'm not going anywhere."

Once Meg had turned off the TV and shuffled Gracie off to the bathroom, Nathan shifted to the couch and opened a magazine. "Fifty Ways to Spruce up Your Kitchen," he mumbled, reading the title of an article he wasn't the least bit interested in.

He was on Tip Number 15 when the bathroom door opened and Gracie bounded out, leaping onto the cushion beside him. She smelled of toothpaste, and her curly hairline was damp where the washcloth had passed. "Good night, Mr. Woods," she said.

Nathan covered his laugh behind a discreet cough.

"It's Mr. Forrest, Gracie," Meg corrected her gently.

"Oh." Gracie thought about her mistake and then giggled until she fell over Nathan's knees. At the feel of that tiny body, his smile stiffened.

"Come on, silly," Meg said, prying Gracie away.

As soon as the bedroom door closed, Nathan let out a breath of relief and returned to the magazine. He flipped a few pages, trying not to listen to the voices in the other room. But in such close quarters, that was impossible. He could hear the coaxing and the balking, the murmurs and the laughter. He could hear Meg reading—*One Fish, Two Fish,* if his memory served him right. But then there was an inexplicable pause.

"Nathan?"

He glanced up, dread seeping into his bones. Meg was standing in the bedroom doorway.

"She won't settle. She really, *really* wants you to see her tent. Do you mind?"

Yes, he did mind. But what could he say?

Nathan hadn't been in a child's room in a long time. He

stepped into this one cautiously, as if it were littered with land mines instead of just toys. He recognized so many of them. The farm animals. The doll house. The rocking horse. The large-size building bricks. Lizzie had had those same playthings, too.

With an effort, he pushed his memories to the back of his mind and said, "So *that's* your tent!"

"Yup!" Gracie was sitting cross-legged inside a nylon dome shaped in the vague design of a car. It covered her bed, which was conveniently low to the floor.

"Very nice," he said.

"No. Come *here* and see it," the child insisted.

Nathan realized he was standing behind a chair, his hands gripping the backrest. He took a deep breath, approached the bed and knelt on the floor, bracing forward on his hands. Inside the colorful dome were a myriad of pillows, dolls and stuffed animals, all arranged around a puffy quilt. It seemed a very cozy nest for a child, something he would've loved himself at Gracie's age.

"Hey, this is neat," he exclaimed with genuine delight.

"Yup. See, there's a window, too."

He glanced upward and indeed saw a window, a small rectangle of clear vinyl to mimic a windshield.

"I wish I had a bed like this."

"Maybe you can get one," Gracie answered logically. "Mommy bought it at a yard sale. Will you read me a story?"

A wave of queasiness rippled through Nathan's stomach.

"We already had stories, Gracie," Meg said, sitting on the floor nearby, arms looped around her knees. Had she sensed his reluctance again?

"Please?" Gracie begged. "Just one?"

"Do you mind?" Meg asked him.

Nathan wiped a hand down his face, ashamed and angry

that a little thing like reading a child's story was getting to him. "Sure," he said with conviction.

Gracie scrambled out of the tent, went to her bookcase, and came back with two books.

"One!" Meg said sternly, stifling a laugh.

"Hmm." Gracie pursed her lips as she studied the two. "Okay. Windy the Pooh." She handed Nathan the chosen book and crawled back into her nest.

He glanced at Meg and mouthed, *"Windy?"* Meg's eyes brimmed with emotions—amusement, pride, love. Oh, yes, lots of love. For an unguarded moment, Nathan basked in the warmth of those emotions, even felt a measure of them himself. Then he opened the book and proceeded with the story.

When he was done, Gracie, of course, asked for another.

"That's all," Meg said firmly. "Which song would you like me to sing?"

"Um. The mountain song." Seeing Nathan making a motion to get up and leave, she cried, "Oh, stay. Puhleease?"

"It won't take more than five minutes," Meg assured him.

He settled again, resting his back against a bedside dresser, and Meg commenced singing, "She'll be coming 'round the mountain when she comes…"

Nathan closed his eyes, listening to Meg's soft voice, trying not to remember other voices, other good-night routines. But the memories were there, burned indelibly into his sense memory. He wanted to get up and leave, wanted to take a long walk, or better yet, a hard run. But he couldn't. It wouldn't be polite. And so he just held tight and endured.

Meg finished the song, but Gracie still wasn't settled. "Can you sing me 'Amazing Grace,' Mr. Forrest?" she asked sweetly.

His eyes snapped open. "Me? You want me to sing?"

"Yes. 'Amazing Grace.'"

"We always finish up with that," Meg explained. She leaned close and whispered in his ear, "She thinks it's about her."

"Oh." But turning to the child, he said, "I'm sorry. I don't know that song." He knew the melody but only some of the words.

"I'll sing it, honey," Meg assured her daughter, then began to do just that.

Gracie lay back immediately, pulling the quilt up to her chin. She sighed contentedly. Relieved to be let off the hook, Nathan relaxed against the bureau again, listening to the lyrics of the old spiritual.

He had to wonder what a three-year-old could possibly like about that particular old hymn, with its references to "wretches" being lost and found. He liked it. He liked it immensely. But a three-year-old?

"I once was lost but now am found, Was blind, but now I see." Meg finished the hymn on an incredibly soft note.

Nathan thought the child was asleep, she lay so still. But then she whispered, "Turn off the light, please."

Nathan looked over his shoulder and snapped off the lamp.

"Now look through here," she whispered, her directive meant unmistakably for him.

"Through where?" he asked, poking his head into the tent.

"Here." Gracie pointed to the vinyl window over her head. "See my stars?"

"Oh, yeah! I do." Nathan was enraptured in spite of himself. He pulled out of the tent and stared up at the ceiling where Meg had attached a heaven of glow-in-the-dark stars.

"Now pick one and make a wish," Gracie instructed, yawning sleepily.

"Okay." Nathan chose a small star with a pinkish glow. But when he tried to make a wish he couldn't think of anything for himself. All his hopes were for Meg and this beautiful, bright, and, yes, amazing Gracie. They deserved better than life had dealt them.

"Good night, love," Meg whispered, leaning into the tent and placing a kiss on her daughter's forehead. Nathan tensed, wondering if he'd be expected to do the same.

"G'night, Mr. Forrest." The words were barely audible. Gracie turned onto her side, her back to him, and cuddled into her pillow. It seemed he was off the hook again. Somehow, though, he didn't feel as pleased as he'd expected.

"Good night, Gracie," he whispered. Then he got up and followed Meg out of the room.

"Would you like a cup of coffee?"

"No, thanks. I should be going. Your mother-in-law is probably having a fit as it is."

Meg's face lost its peacefulness and became troubled again, as it had been when he'd first arrived.

"Meg, what we were talking about before, your wanting to move into your own place... Do you have a plan? A specific amount of money you need to save?"

She nodded. "Yes, as a matter of fact, I do."

"Would you be offended if I asked you to discuss it with me?"

"No. I guess not." She opened a kitchen drawer and came back to the sitting area with a spiral notebook. Nathan sat beside her as she opened the notebook on her knees. In small neat handwriting she'd listed her take-home pay and subtracted monthly expenses. Then she'd enumerated what she was aiming to save: a disturbingly small figure for initial apartment expenses, a furniture budget that convinced him she planned to shop at Good Will, and a car price that put her in a near-wreck category.

"Is that a down payment for a car or the full price you expect to pay?"

"Oh, the full price. I don't have any collateral, so I doubt I'll be able to get a loan."

Nathan went back to examining the list. She'd written *baby-sitter* and punctuated it with three question marks.

"I'm not sure Vera will want to baby-sit after I move out. She may be too upset with me. But even if she does, she'll probably start charging."

"And you wouldn't have Gracie stay with anyone else?"

"I'm still hoping to find a preschool for her, but beyond that? No. I don't know anybody else."

"And what's this last entry? Bus fare to St Louis?"

The color in her cheeks deepened. "I added that one night in a fit of…" She paused. "On a whim. I considered moving back to the town where I grew up."

"Do you still want to go?"

"No. I like Providence."

Sometimes she just wanted to put half a continent between her and her in-laws, Nathan thought, that was all. He took the notebook from her and sat back, glancing down her monthly expenses column, then at her "goal" column. "How long do you think it'll take you to reach this goal?"

"At the rate I'm going, forever. It seems as soon as I get a little ahead something comes up to pull me back."

Some*thing* or some*one?*

"Seriously, if all goes smoothly," she continued, "I figure four, maybe five months."

Nathan studied the figures, figures so small to him he could've written her a check right then and there out of his daily expenses account. But Meg had too much pride. He already knew she wouldn't take a loan.

But surely there was some other way he could help her

reach her goals faster. Before long, an idea began to take form.

"Maggie Mae, I think this is going to work out better than I thought."

"What is?" She looked at him cautiously.

"I didn't come over here just to apologize, although that was my primary motive. I wanted to discuss a business proposition with you, too." He remembered his remark on the stairs outside, that he needed to talk to her about her job, and thought: Wasn't that a stroke of luck! "Within the next couple of months I can foresee several occasions when I'll need your personal assistance again."

"You mean, like last weekend?"

"Yes, sort of." He wished he knew where he was going with this.

She chewed on the corner of her lip. "I won't work more than my usual forty-hour week. As much as I need the money, I have to spend time with Gracie."

Nathan rubbed his jaw, thinking fast. "I wouldn't expect you to. If you worked a Saturday, say, you could take off a different day of the week. We could explore doing work at home, too."

Meg still looked uncertain. "What extra jobs do you have in mind?"

"Oh, all sorts of things." Nathan combed his mind. "There's a trade show coming up in a month, for example. I could use you then, anything from setting up our display to meeting with clients when I can't."

"Meeting with clients?" Her brows knit.

"Yes. It seems you did quite a good job with my cousin Curt. This week he called in an order so large I had to ask him if he was joking."

Meg's face lit up. "Really?"

"Really. He said you were knowledgeable and very efficient. He also told me I should pay you a commission."

Meg laughed. "Anything else?"

"Oh, sure. There are lots of other little jobs nobody seems to have the time to do," he said vaguely before homing in on the favor he really had come here to ask her about. "There's one in particular I'm desperate for you to do."

"Oh? What?"

"My parents are coming into town next Saturday and want to take us out to dinner." He watched her expressions change, shifting from puzzlement to awareness, through shock into anxiety.

"Ah, I see. The charade continues."

He knew he looked chagrined. "How about it, Meg? One more time?"

"Nathan." She tilted her head and gave him a scolding look. "Don't you think it's time you leveled with them? Such behavior from a grown man—it seems rather silly."

Nathan chewed on the inside of his cheek. He'd been hoping to avoid telling Meg about Rachel and Lizzie, but it bothered him that she thought he had nothing more serious to do in his spare time than play childish games with his parents.

"I don't know quite how to approach this," he began slowly. "And believe me, I've given it a lot of thought. So I'll just dive in and tell you. I used to be married, Meg. I used to have a daughter, too."

CHAPTER SEVEN

MEG didn't move, not by an eyelash, yet she felt as if a tornado had lifted her off the sofa and twirled her around a few million times. "You were married?" she exclaimed. "You had a daughter?"

Nathan nodded grimly. "I can see from your expression that this is news to you." Meg could only nod. "Not many people at the factory know, and those who do, understand that I prefer it not be discussed."

"What happened? Are you divorced?"

"No, Maggie Mae." He sighed. "We have more in common than you realize." In a voice so matter-of-fact he might have been dictating a business letter, he added, "My wife and daughter died in a plane crash."

Meg sucked in her breath. "Oh, God! How awful, Nathan. I'm so sorry."

His face remained set. He seemed determined to avoid emotionalism, but she could see from the tension around his eyes that the subject was paining him.

"When did it happen?"

"Five years ago. We were living in Wisconsin at the time, in Rachel's home town, but we'd come East to visit my folks for a week. At the end of the week I decided to stay on a while longer to discuss taking over the jewelry factory with my father. But Rachel needed to get home."

"And it was that flight?"

"Yes." Despite his determination to deliver the information without emotion, Nathan looked forlorn. He probably didn't even realize it, but Meg could see the misery in his eyes. She wished she could comfort him somehow, but she felt words were meaningless, and what she wanted to do—take him in her arms—seemed inappropriate.

He drew up his shoulders, apparently finding his own solace. "At least they died instantly, I'm told. They didn't know a moment's pain."

"That's something." Derek had survived half a day. But rather than get into that, she said, "What was your daughter's name?" She kicked off her shoes and folded her legs under her, facing him at her end of the sofa.

"Elizabeth. Lizzie," he added with a melancholy smile. "She was almost three when she died."

"Almost Gracie's age."

"Yes." Nathan leaned forward, his elbows braced on his knees, and ran his two index fingers over the edge of the coffee table. "Her and Rachel's deaths changed my life. Changed *me*. We'd been very happy, the three of us. A perfect little family. When they died, part of me died, too— the part that was husband and father."

He sat up and turned to face Meg more directly. "What's left is someone quite different, someone who's not interested in family life. I enjoy the company of women. I enjoy socializing. But I have no intention of ever getting serious again."

As he spoke, Meg felt herself growing despondent, stricken in a way she didn't understand. Or maybe she did and just didn't want to face it.

"That's why my mother's intervention bothers me so much. It isn't the cute, innocent game of matchmaking it appears on the surface. She's trying to force me past my loss, get me to heal. That's her real agenda. The fact she refuses to accept, though, is that just isn't me anymore. She's working on a lost cause."

Meg's heart ached. A lost cause? Was he really? "Lots of people make new lives for themselves after tragedy," she offered.

One dark eyebrow arched, questioning her silently.

"Sure," she said, "I wouldn't mind getting married again someday."

"You wouldn't feel you were betraying your first husband?"

"Uh-uh. I consider my willingness to take another chance a compliment to Derek. If we had been unhappy, I might not be so willing."

"An interesting point."

"Mostly, though, it'd be good for Gracie. She was less than a year old when Derek died. She doesn't have a clue what real family life is like."

"You're doing an excellent job with her all on your own."

"Thanks. But it's not the same as having a father around. Fathers add a whole other dimension to a child's development. I'd also like to have another child or two, provide Gracie a few siblings." She smiled. "I can't do that on my own."

They'd both been sitting with an arm draped along the back of the sofa. Now Nathan moved a little closer and covered her hand with his. "I hope that happens for you, Meg. I hope all your dreams come true. But we're not all cut from the same cloth. Please don't expect me to want the same. Be a friend and don't expect that of me." The moment felt raw, honest, their innermost needs out in the open.

Meg turned her hand over so that their palms touched, warmly, intimately, and, though her heart ached, she agreed with one word, "Friend."

He held her hand tightly. "Thanks."

After a while she pulled away, smiling at a sudden insight. "Boy, what a pair we make. You with a mother who's trying to get you to move on in life, and me with a mother-in-law who wants to keep me stuck in the past!"

Nathan smiled until the dimple in his right cheek appeared. "You're right, Meg. Fortunately, neither of them is going to succeed, because you and I are going to help each other." Those damnable sapphire eyes drilled into her. "Right?"

She remembered he was still waiting for her answer regarding dinner with his parents. "Do you mind if I sleep on it?"

He sighed. "If you must."

"Yes, I must," she teased. "I'll let you know Monday."

Nathan glanced at his watch. "Well, I really should be going." They got up and started for the door.

"What are you doing tomorrow, now that you're not planning to go to New Hampshire?"

"Oh, let's see. I think I'll take Gracie to Roger Williams Zoo. I've been promising to for a while." She opened the door and stepped out on the landing with Nathan. "What a lovely night."

"Yes. Very mild." He moved to start down the stairs.

"Oh, wait." Meg touched his arm. "I thought you wanted to explain your behavior this week. You know—" she smiled "—the reason you were such a brute with me."

Nathan gazed up at the night sky a moment, his eyes traveling skittishly. "The extra jobs. They're the reason. I've wanted to ask you to be my special assistant for some time, but I was afraid last weekend had spoiled any new working relationship we might attempt. Things got a little heated last Saturday, and I imagined...well, I imagined a lot of things, everything from your quitting in disgust to your believing more had happened than actually did. I was afraid I'd lost you as a secretary and was angry at myself for creating the situation."

"I see. Well, I hope our conversation tonight has put an end to your concerns."

"It has. I feel a lot better now that I know where you're

coming from. Thanks for being so open and understanding."

"Likewise."

Meg wished he could value her less as a secretary and more as a woman. Still, friendship with Nathan was a development beyond anything she could have imagined when she'd first started working for him. She would try to be satisfied with that.

Meg was packing a picnic lunch the next morning, and feeling newly energetic and optimistic, when her phone rang.

"Hi, Meg. It's Tina," came a cheery voice.

Meg had been thinking about Nathan's sister all week. She'd had the urge to call her but feared Tina might feel she was being presumptuous about their friendship. As they talked, though, Meg realized her fears had been unfounded. In fact, Tina had felt the same trepidation.

When Tina revealed that she knew about Meg's marriage and daughter, Meg was relieved. She'd disliked deceiving Tina. Similarly, Tina was pleased to hear that Nathan had visited and told her about his past.

"It explains so much," Meg said. "I couldn't figure out why he was so uneasy with my daughter. Now I understand. It must be really hard for him to be around children."

"True. But it also explains why he was so aloof with you this week." Meg had touched briefly on that subject, too.

"I'm afraid I don't follow. The reason for that was, he thought our work relationship had been damaged by the weekend we spent at Beechcroft."

"And you believed it?" Tina exclaimed. "Meg, honey, the reason my brother gave you a hard time this week has nothing to do with a work relationship. He's made it a policy to date only women who aren't interested in marriage, women who don't have kids and never *want* to have kids. He avoids the rest of our gender like the plague.''

"Yes, I know. So?"

"So, last weekend he got out-maneuvered by his own policy because he fell for you.''

"Oh, I don't think so."

"I do. Nathan was thinking of asking you out. I'd bet my last dime on it. But then he met your daughter and realized he couldn't. You were in that category of women he considered undatable. *That's* why he retreated from you at work. *That's* why he was so cool and aloof.''

"Cool and aloof? He was a beast!"

"Just goes to show how disappointed he was.''

Meg was still reluctant to get her hopes up. "It was purely a business concern, a case of fearing he'd lost a good secretary.''

"You could be right—but I doubt it.''

They moved on to talking about preparations for Tina's wedding, and before either of them realized it an hour had passed.

"My goodness, but we can talk!" Meg exclaimed.

"And I haven't even got warmed up yet. Can I interest you in lunch sometime this week? There's a great little restaurant on Thayer Street I've been dying to try.''

Meg smiled. Her life was changing. Last night after she'd talked to Vera and gotten that repair bill, she'd felt she was deluding herself. But she really was on the move. She had a lunch date with a friend, and that hadn't happened since she was eighteen.

But, of course, a more significant change was that she now had Nathan in her corner actively helping her. He was the reason for the optimism and energy coursing through her today.

"That'd be great, Tina. Is Thursday good for you?"

"Thursday's wonderful. I have to go into the city for a

fitting anyway. Tell you what. I'll swing by the factory at noon and pick you up.''

''Thanks. See you then.''

Meg had brought Gracie to the Roger Williams Park Zoo only once previous to this trip, so that everything was relatively new to her. She was clearly enraptured. It was a beautifully designed zoo, and Meg walked along wrapped in her own kind of enchantment.

They delighted in watching a train of elephants taking a stroll under their keeper's careful eye, each animal holding onto the tail of the one in front with his trunk. They fed the sheep in the petting zoo, made faces at the mischievous monkeys, and were charmed by a baby giraffe cavorting with his mother.

Gracie especially enjoyed the prairie dog exhibit. By crawling through an entrance similar to a large sewer pipe, they reached an underground chamber with several Plexiglas domes in the ceiling. The domes made it possible for a person to pop up, just like a prairie dog, and take a peek at the outside world.

Meg lifted Gracie, since the bubbles were a little too high for her. ''Look, honey, we can see outside.''

Her daughter squealed as a small animal scooted by at eye level. ''A perry dog!''

''Yup. There are lots of them. See? And over there, that's the path we were walking on.''

''Yup, I see. And over there, there's Mr. Forrest.''

''What!'' Meg swiveled in the direction Gracie was looking. She was right. Nathan was walking along the path, his head turning as if he was searching for something. Suddenly an already pleasant day turned golden.

''Hey!'' Gracie called and waved her arms. ''Hi! Hi!''

Nathan's eyes turned their way. He frowned, stepped closer, frowned harder—and then threw back his head and laughed. Watching him, Meg couldn't help laughing, too. What a sight she and Gracie must appear from his viewpoint, just their heads showing within this bubble at ground level!

She crawled out, her daughter ahead of her. Her heart was doing cartwheels. "Hi. What are you doing here?" she asked, brushing off her knees.

"Looking for you." His eyes glittered as they traveled over her. "Hey, you're wearing jeans! And your hair's in a ponytail."

"It's Saturday. What did you expect? Another suit?"

"Yes. No. I don't know. I…I'm all turned around." He chuckled. "Have you been here long?"

"Less than an hour. Why?"

"Just wondering if I could join you. Do you mind?"

"Of course not," she replied, happiness flowing through her. Nathan looked different today, too. It wasn't just the jeans and sweatshirt he was wearing. She'd seen him in casual clothes before. It was that he seemed more relaxed. He even looked younger.

"Is there a reason for this unexpected pleasure?" she asked.

He shrugged. "I was on my way to the factory, thinking I might catch up on a few things, when I said to myself, 'Nathan, are you out of your mind? Today is Saturday, and the weather's gorgeous. You should be out enjoying it.' So here I am."

Meg knew he belonged to a country club and could be out playing golf. He also kept a boat at a nearby yacht club and could be sailing. Or he could be horseback riding at his parents' estate. Yet he'd chosen to come to the zoo?

Tina's comment about his being interested in her returned. She glanced up at his handsome face, speculating. It couldn't be!

"I have to admit there's another reason that brought me here—the work I was hoping to catch up on today."

Meg's heart sank. Right, it *couldn't* be.

"I was wondering if you'd consider taking it on as your first extra assignment. It isn't difficult, just tedious. It involves tabulating the results of a survey I sent to the salesmen out in the field—what's selling, what's not, their opinions why and suggestions for improvement. It's a job you can probably do at home." He then named a sum he was willing to pay her. She accepted on the spot.

"Great. Now, can I coerce you into also accepting the dinner invitation with my parents?" He leaned in, turning up the charm.

"You said I could sleep on it."

"You have."

Meg was ready to object that he'd given her till Monday, but Gracie, meanwhile, had been tugging on his hand, pleading with him to crawl into the prairie dog exhibit.

"Gracie, enough!" Meg warned.

"Oh, it's all right." Nathan ruffled the child's curls. "I always did want to know what it was like to live in a burrow."

He followed Gracie through the pipe and a moment later appeared in one of the bubbles. He looked around, searching for Meg, and when he found her he grinned. It was a smile that reached deep inside her, touching something vital and feminine—and neglected far too long.

Apparently the problem of dinner with his parents was still on his mind, because he clasped his hands as if he were praying and mouthed the word *Please?,* his eyes so endearingly pathetic that she burst out laughing.

"All right, I'll go," she called. If he heard her indistinctly, he at least got her drift. Blowing two-handed kisses her way, he mouthed, "Thank you."

"I'll go under one condition," Meg said when he'd emerged and they'd started up the walking path.

"Bargaining for a raise already?"

"No, not a raise. I want you to agree we'll tell your parents the truth, that we're not really dating."

He looked at her drolly. "That sort of defeats the purpose of your being there, don't you think?"

Meg remained firm. "You want me to help you, right? You want your mother's matchmaking to stop?"

"Ye-ah," he answered dubiously.

"Then, let's be honest with her. Once she realizes the extremes you went to just to avoid her interference, she'll understand how out-of-line she was and stop."

"You think so, huh?"

"Yes, I do."

Entering the polar bear exhibit, Gracie made a beeline for the large viewing window where three magnificent white bears were swimming on the other side.

"It's for your own good, Nathan. Your sister called this morning, and as we talked I realized how relieved I was that she knew the truth about me. I realized how burdensome deceptions are, how complicated they make our lives."

She and Nathan stepped closer to the tank. Gracie was giggling at the antics of a cub, tumbling right in front of her.

"Oh, all right. We'll 'fess up." He sighed. "From now on, there'll be no more deceptions."

After returning to the car for the picnic hamper, Meg spread a blanket under a tree and laid out their lunch. She was glad she'd packed extra. It was a simple meal. There was no champagne today, no smoked salmon or butter pats shaped like flowers—only egg salad sandwiches and lemonade, with grapes and oatmeal cookies for dessert. But

Nathan didn't seem to mind. In fact, he even cleaned up what Gracie didn't eat.

After lunch they strolled through the park, admiring the carefully planted flower beds. They rented a paddleboat and explored the pond. They rode the antique carousel and bought Gracie a big red balloon. By then she was beginning to fade, though, and Meg suggested it was time to go home.

"You were great with her today," she told Nathan after he'd helped strap Gracie into her car seat.

"I hope so," he said, holding the car door open for Meg. "She was another reason I wanted to join you today. It's one thing for me not to want children of my own, but quite another to be tense around other people's kids. There's no excuse for it."

Was he using Gracie to learn to loosen up with children? Had this lovely day been merely a therapy session to him? Meg found herself irked by that thought. She wished he could have enjoyed Gracie simply for who she was.

"Glad we could be of service," she replied with a touch of sarcasm. If he caught it, it didn't show.

"By the way," he said, "I really like how you look today."

She was still too annoyed to enjoy the compliment. But as he strolled off, heading toward his own car across the lot, she thought his step seemed lighter than usual. He was whistling, too. The tune was flat and sporadic, but Meg was still able to recognize it. It was the hymn "Amazing Grace."

"Glad to be of service," she repeated. This time she meant every syllable.

It wasn't until the next day while she and Gracie were at the Gilberts having Sunday dinner that Meg realized she'd accepted Nathan's invitation to go out with his parents without arranging baby-sitting first.

"What are you doing next Saturday night?" she asked, cutting up Gracie's pork chop.

"Oh, just the usual," Vera replied, heaping her husband's plate with mashed potatoes. The "usual" meant they'd be watching TV for four hours. "Why?"

With heightened trepidation, Meg asked if they'd watch Gracie. Predictably, Vera wanted to know the reason. Meg couldn't think of anything but the truth.

"You're going out to dinner with that Forrest fella?"

Meg's pulse raced at the narrowing of Vera's eyes. "It's a business dinner." It *was,* she told herself. In agreeing to help each other, she and Nathan *had* made a deal—of sorts.

Vera's grilling went on for several more minutes. So did the eloquent glances between her and her husband. Finally, though, they agreed to baby-sit, but Meg was wiped out.

Vera needed the car on Monday, so Meg got dropped off at work. She was just crossing to the entrance when Nathan swung his own car into the slot with his name on it. He signaled for her to wait.

"I need to talk to you," he said as they crossed the foyer to the elevator.

"What about?"

"In a moment," he whispered. Several other office personnel were riding the elevator with them, and their curiosity was glaring. As of Friday Meg and Mr. Forrest had been on the outs. Now they were standing together, arms pressing, tight as ticks.

Inside his office he raised the blinds, turned on the radio to a classical station and poured two cups of freshly brewed coffee, waiting on a hot plate in the next room.

"Have a seat, Meg," he said, handing her a cup.

After taking a sip, she rested the cup on her knee. "What did you want to discuss?"

Nathan settled into his big leather chair. "I hope you won't be offended, but I called a friend of mine who happens to be the headmaster at a place called Bishop Academy. Are you familiar with it?''

Meg nodded. ''A private elementary school, right?''

''Yes. This year; though, they're adding a preschool section.''

Meg's pulse jumped. ''Oh, yes?''

''Mm.'' Nathan was having trouble containing a smile. ''And my friend said he'd be pleased to have Gracie as a student.''

Meg gasped. ''That's wonderful!'' But her joy faded immediately.

Nathan understood. ''You're not obliged to follow up on my inquiry, Meg. I realize the tuition at Bishop may be more than you'd counted on paying. But it isn't *that* steep, and the attention Gracie would get there would be top-notch.''

''Not too heavily into academics, I hope.''

''Oh, no. It's all directed play. Classes start this Wednesday, though, so if you want Gracie enrolled, you'll have to call back today. They'll hold open a place for her until six o'clock. After that, they'll give it to someone else.''

Meg was sure she'd have to decline. But then Nathan casually added, ''Oh, by the way, I've left instructions with Mrs. Xavier to compute the sales commission on Curt's order and to cut you a check in that amount.''

Meg's eyes widened. ''I thought you were kidding.''

''Business is business, Meg.'' He got to his feet, handing her the number for the school. ''Don't feel pressured. You have all day to…''

''I accept! Yes! I don't need another minute. She's going!'' Meg shot from the chair, laughing, and gave Nathan a quick hug—but not so quick that she didn't appreciate his clean, crisp morning scent. ''Thank you. Thank you,'' she said.

His parting laughter stayed with her the rest of the day.

On Tuesday Meg came into work deflated, however. Vera had thought the idea of sending Gracie to Bishop Academy senseless. "Have you considered how much driving around that's going to require?" she'd complained. "And I'm the one who's going to have to do it. There'll be dropping you off at work, then dropping Grace off at school, picking her up at one, and four hours later leaving the house again to pick *you* up."

Meg hadn't considered that. Hadn't considered the wear and tear on the car, either, until Jay reminded her.

"What you need is a car of your own," Nathan said. Meg was sitting with him in his office again, same as the day before, the morning sun gleaming on the city beyond his window. "Then you could take her back and forth to school yourself."

"How? I'd have to leave work."

He shrugged casually. "I make allowances for other employees with kids."

Once again hope began to lift her flattened spirits. "Yikes, I've never bought a car before."

He smiled. "Afraid the salesmen'll see how green you are?"

"Among other things."

Nathan glanced at his watch, then buzzed Mrs. Xavier. "Agnes, Ms. Gilbert will be away from the office for part of the morning. So will I."

No questions were asked. "Thank you," was the only remark the woman made.

Nathan took Meg to a used-car dealer who, he said, had a solid reputation. Before long she had a sizeable list of possibilities, cars that were in reliable running order and whose monthly payments she could afford, *if* she could get a loan. To find that out, Nathan encouraged her to discuss financing with the salesman.

"Do you have anyone who'll cosign the loan," the sales-man asked when he realized she had no credit history. She thought of the Gilberts but was reluctant to get them in-volved. She already knew they'd discourage this purchase. They'd see it as one more step away from them—and they'd be right.

"I'll cosign," Nathan offered.

Meg's anxiety level was second only to her sense of wonder. Was there no end to this man's kindness? "I can't let you do that," she whispered out of the corner of her mouth.

"I insist. In fact, let's do all the paperwork right now so I don't have to come back. When you get up the courage to choose a car, you can just come down here on your own and do it."

Then, turning to the salesman, "Make sure she gets something dependable, too." Nathan's look was sharp. "The car you sell her's going to be carrying precious cargo."

The man nodded. "I hear ya."

So did Meg. She'd never felt such stern protectiveness in a man before, not even in Derek.

"The reason I wanted to set everything up," he ex-plained on the drive back to work, "I'm going to be gone most of next week."

"You are?" The magnitude of Meg's dismay startled her.

"Mm. There's a trade show I have to attend in Chicago. So be careful. If I were buying the car, I'd go with either that blue Taurus or the red Saturn."

Meg nodded, feeling the mantle of his protectiveness again.

The next morning Meg wangled the Escort from Vera—it was becoming harder to do—and drove Gracie to her first session of preschool. That afternoon she received her check for tabulating the results of Nathan's survey and deposited it in her savings account. That evening Nathan had her come by his condominium to pick up another task. She took Gracie with her.

"And how did you enjoy your first day of school?" Nathan asked. They were sitting in the living room of a surprisingly modest apartment. It was tasteful, comfortable, but mostly just functional.

"School was grrreat!" Gracie jumped to punctuate her remark.

Nathan laughed. "In that case..." He reached for a gift bag and handed it to her. "I guess you'll be needing this."

Gracie took the bag eagerly and pulled out a lunch box with a picture of The Little Mermaid on it. Her face lit up. "Oh, my!" she exclaimed.

Barely containing his amusement, Nathan looked at Meg, sitting on the couch beside him, and mouthed, "Oh, my?" behind his hand. Smiling, she just shrugged.

"Thank you, Mr. Forrest." Gracie wound her arms around his neck and squeezed. Meg noticed him stiffen at first, but then he relaxed and hugged her in return.

"My pleasure, Gracie," he said.

At noon on Thursday, Tina came by the factory as planned and picked Meg up for lunch. They were sitting in a trendy café on the East Side near Brown University, munching on thick deli sandwiches and discussing Meg's upcoming dinner date, when Tina said, "You're nervous, aren't you?"

"Gee, how can you tell?" Meg held her hand over the table and let it shake.

"But why? You spent a whole weekend with my folks."

"Nathan and I plan to tell them the truth."

"About the charade?"

"Yes."

"Aw, heck, Meg." Tina threw down a potato chip she'd been about to pop into her mouth.

"Why are you so disappointed?"

"I like you two dating, no matter what the reason." She shrugged. "Ah, well, maybe he'll start asking you out on his own."

Meg rolled her eyes. "I'm having enough difficulty coping with his friendship, Tina."

"Difficulty how? Trying to hide the fact that you wish it were more?"

Meg pressed her hands to her face. Her cheeks were warming. "Let's talk about something else. Please?"

Tina chuckled. "Sure—for now." She took a bite of her sandwich, chewed it and swallowed. "I have a favor to ask. Please don't feel you have to say yes. I realize I'm asking at the last minute."

"What is it?"

"Will you be a bridesmaid at my wedding?"

Meg sat dumbfounded, coffee cup pressed to her lips.

"The gown is already ordered and paid for, so you won't have any extra expense. One of my friends has had to drop out of the bridal party, and I'd be grateful and really honored if you'd take her place."

Even a week earlier Meg would have declined, but not today. This was a week of change. She was riding something positive and forward-thrusting, and she would *not* interrupt the flow. "I'd love to," she replied. "Tell me what I need to do."

While they finished their meal, they discussed her gown and alterations, as well as the rehearsal dinner. It was almost time for Meg to return to work when Tina added, "There's one more thing you have to do—clear your calendar a week from Saturday."

"Why? What's happening then?"

"I'm piling you and the other bridesmaids into my car

and taking you to Newbury Street in Boston for a day of pampering. Hair, nails, massage—whatever you girls want." At Meg's quizzical expression, she laughed. "It's traditional for a bride to give her attendants a gift, right? Well, that's mine."

Meg gazed at Tina askance. "That's awfully…generous."

"I have to go for myself anyway. I need to get my hair trimmed and do a makeup run-through. The other two girls've already agreed to go along. How about you, Meg? Will you make it a party?"

Meg threw up her hands with a smile of surrender. "Sure. Why not?" Why not, indeed? It was a week for change.

Eventually Saturday evening arrived—and time for another change, disabusing the Forrests of the idea that she and Nathan were a couple.

Meg was on tenterhooks as she got ready. She applied her makeup with extra care and curled her hair in hot rollers, something she never did. She'd thought to wear it loose and swinging about her shoulders, but when she took the curlers out, it looked a fright. It puffed too much, overwhelming her face, and so she resorted to pinning it up again.

Dabbing on her cologne she noticed her hands were trembling. *What's the matter with you, Margaret Mary?* she chided herself. She was acting as if this was a real date, when in actuality it was just the opposite. Tonight's mission was to tell the Forrests that she and Nathan were *not* going together.

"Does this dress look okay to you, Gracie?" Meg was wearing her best, a jade-colored silk that draped and swirled as softly as a cloud—a designer creation she'd found at the Salvation Army when she'd gone shopping for play clothes for her daughter.

Standing beside her at the full-length mirror, Gracie nodded solemnly. "You look beautiful."

Meg had her doubts. She took off her glasses and
squinted at her fuzzy image, wondering if she could survive
the night without them. She groaned. Now was not the time
to try. She'd undoubtedly end up salting her food with pepper and buttering her wrist instead of her bread.

Nathan came by for her at quarter to seven, with Vera
fast on his heels—although to be honest Meg hardly noticed her mother-in-law. Her eyes filled with Nathan as
soon as he walked in the door. Dressed in a suit of dark
gray worsted, worn with a pearl-gray shirt and red paisley
tie, he looked good enough to serve for dessert.

Nathan's parents met them at a restaurant on Federal Hill
that had won national acclaim for its authentic Italian cui-
sine.

"How lovely you look tonight," Edmund said, kissing
Meg's cheek.

"It's so nice to see you again," Pia said, giving her a
hug. Meg cast Nathan a glance, silently telling him not to
keep these wonderful people in the dark too long.

He didn't. They'd just finished their soup and were waiting for their main course, when he explained the situation.
His parents were stunned. It took both him and Meg to
convince them their relationship was merely professional,
although they did confess to a sideline friendship.

Mrs. Forrest was particularly disappointed. "It seemed
too good to be true," she said so quietly that only Meg
heard.

Nathan took a sip of his wine, set the glass down. "I
hope you finally realize how much your matchmaking bothered me, Mother."

"I do, and I feel terrible. To think you felt you had to
go to such lengths to protect yourself." She caught her
lower lip in her teeth. "I'm sorry. It won't happen again."

Meg caught Nathan's eye, her look saying, *See? I told you!* He returned a small concessionary grin.

Bringing her attention back to the older couple, she said, "I'm sorry I deceived you. It bothered me the entire time I was at your house."

A smile warmed Mrs. Forrest's pretty face. "Don't waste another minute worrying about it, Meg. Let's use the time, instead, getting to know one another."

It turned out to be a lovely evening, not at all the stressful confrontation Meg had anticipated. The Forrests were delighted to hear about Gracie, especially when Nathan added anecdotes from his own experiences with her.

"Well, I'll be!" Edmund exclaimed quietly. He seemed to be saying that all night, his sharp gaze moving constantly from Meg to Nathan.

When Meg got home later that night, a note was waiting on the kitchen table, informing her that Gracie was sleeping over at the Gilberts'. After reading the note, she turned to thank Nathan for the evening.

He beat her to it. "Thanks for helping me out, Meg. I think my mother's learned her lesson and won't be bothering me anymore."

"Mm. I think so, too."

"I wish I knew *how* to thank you, but we didn't discuss compensation for this particular…"

"Don't insult me." Meg cast him a reproachful look. "I had a great time. That was compensation enough."

It was clearly time to say good-night, but neither of them seemed in a hurry. With his eyes intent on her, Nathan took hold of a flyaway curl and tried tucking it into her back-swept hairdo. It slipped right out again. "I enjoyed the evening, too," he said softly.

Meg shivered as the back of his fingers brushed along her jawline. She glanced aside. "Um—when are you leaving for Chicago?"

"Tomorrow." He leaned his shoulder against the door close to her, making the atmosphere even more intimate.

"So soon?" Meg feared her disappointment was showing.

"Yes. Till next Friday."

I'll miss you, she thought.

"Have you made a decision about buying a car?"

"Yes. I'm going to speak to the dealer Monday."

"Don't forget, there'll be insurance and registration fees."

She nodded. "I've got the money put aside." She dared a look up into his eyes, wondering what was happening between them. They were discussing neutral matters, but the mood didn't feel neutral. Not to her, anyway. The very air between them was vibrating with sexual energy, charged with a special excitement.

Within the next heartbeat it hit her. She was falling in love with Nathan. What she felt was no longer just a harmless crush. This was love—beautiful, crazy, all-consuming love.

Painful love, because it had nowhere to go.

She had to stop thinking of Nathan in romantic terms. The only reason she was able to enjoy such an evening as this was that he believed a romance between them was *not* possible.

And it wasn't. Their goals in life were diametrically opposed. He wanted to remain single; she dreamed of marriage. He didn't want children; she already had a child and would count herself blessed to have another. On top of all that, they were boss and employee!

"Well, I really should say good-night," Nathan murmured.

Taking a deep breath, she nodded and reached for the door. But then they paused and glanced at each other. She was in his arms before she knew it.

It's only a hug, she told herself. *It's nothing romantic, nothing sexual. Just a hug between friends.* But that hug was long and tight, and she could feel him all down the length of her, his hardness and his warmth.

"Take care of yourself," he said, his arms tightening before he released her.

"You too." She touched his cheek in place of a kiss.

He stepped back awkwardly, pushed his hand through his hair, then turned abruptly and hurried down the stairs.

Meg slumped into a kitchen chair when he was gone. Tonight had been dedicated to honesty, to dismantling the ruse that she and Nathan were a couple. No more pretenses—that was their new policy.

Well, guess what, that policy wasn't working. She might have helped put an end to one charade tonight, but in claiming she wasn't interested in Nathan, she'd entered another!

CHAPTER EIGHT

NATHAN knew something had gone wrong with his and Meg's relationship the following night when he was unpacking his bag in his hotel room in Chicago. He'd forgotten the small bifold frame he always included when he traveled, his pictures of Rachel and Lizzie. Five years of business trips, and he'd never before forgotten.

He stood at the luggage rack, staring into his empty suitcase, remembering how distracted he'd been while packing. He'd been thinking about Meg, about how soft and pretty she'd looked at dinner the previous evening, bathed in candlelight. He'd been recalling how she'd felt in his arms later, saying goodbye at her door.

He closed the suitcase, sat back on the bed and thought, *Nathan, you're in deep trouble.*

For the past two weeks he'd been living under the delusion he had his attraction to Meg under control. He'd also believed that attraction would dissipate of its own frailty. Instead, it had only grown stronger, and his control was hanging on by a thread.

He didn't know what he was going to do. He knew what he *wanted* to do—and it wasn't settling for awkward, brotherly hugs when they said good-night.

Nathan scrubbed at his head and emitted a sound that was half groan, half laugh. "What the hell," he muttered, grinning. "Why not go for it?"

A relationship with Meg would be new territory for him. She was an employee. But more importantly, she came with expectations he couldn't fill. As with their friendship, they'd be making up the rules as they went along. Still, their friendship seemed to be doing okay. Why not attempt this, too?

Nathan breathed a relieved sigh. He was going to do it. When he got back he'd have a talk with her. He'd remind her that marriage and kids weren't on the agenda, and the only thing he could offer was a temporary relationship. But then he'd tell her how much he wanted that relationship, how wonderful he thought it would be, and ask her to help him work out the details.

He was fairly certain she'd agree. She was just getting back into circulation. Surely she'd be content simply to date for a while. She couldn't expect every man she met to automatically be interested in marrying her.

Nathan already knew one of the first things they'd do as an honest couple. His cousin Curt had called yesterday to remind him he'd be in town next Saturday. They'd make it a foursome, once he found Curt a date. He glanced at the phone. Maybe he should call Meg and have that talk with her now.

Somehow, though, discussing something that important on the phone didn't seem right. He'd wait. In the meantime, he needed to get some sleep. Come morning, he had clients to meet.

Change continued to mark Meg's days while Nathan was gone. On Monday after work, she and Gracie went to the used-car lot and bought themselves a car, a zippy red four-door sedan. She didn't tell the Gilberts until the purchase was a *fait accompli*, though, because she knew what they'd say. And they did.

But, Meg, you can't afford it! But, Meg, it's so unnecessary; you know you can use our cars: What condition is it in? Why didn't you have Jay check it out? What got into you? Don't you trust us anymore?

Actually, Meg didn't. She was beginning to notice things

amiss in her apartment. Not small unimportant things, like misplaced dishes. Small *important* things like her bankbook and a copy of her credit-card application. When she'd gone looking for them earlier in the day, they'd been in the wrong pockets of the accordion file where she kept her financial papers.

She refused to let that sully her enthusiasm, though. She loved her little red car, and she was sure that buying it was the right decision.

On Tuesday Meg allowed another change into her life when she went for her annual eye exam and asked the optometrist if contact lenses were a viable choice with her particular eye problem.

"They sure are," the doctor answered. And so Meg took the plunge and ordered a pair.

On Wednesday morning she learned about a possible extra baby-sitter for Gracie. Mrs. Xavier's sister had retired from a twenty-year career as a nanny and was looking for clients. "I know you have your mother-in-law," Mrs. Xavier said, "but just in case you're ever in a bind, here's Myrth's card. She's incredible with kids."

And the changes didn't stop there. Later that same morning Meg looked up from her computer to find Curt Forrest smiling down at her. "Curt! My goodness, what a surprise!"

"Hello, Meg."

She'd forgotten what a good-looking man he was. Or perhaps she hadn't noticed in the first place because during that weekend at the Forrests' he'd had Nathan to compete with.

"What are you doing here?"

"Come to take a beautiful lady to lunch. Is one available?" His hazel eyes twinkled merrily. Virtually every other female in the business office was ignoring her work and admiring him instead.

"Maybe," Meg said on a laugh. "It depends on where you're offering to take her."

"Anywhere her heart desires."

Meg dropped the levity. "Curt, are you serious?"

"Yes, ma'am."

She bit her lip, weighing the whys and wherefores of this unexpected invitation. He'd probably intended to go to lunch with Nathan but, finding him gone, was making do with her.

"I don't get off for another half hour," she said.

"Just enough time to take me on a tour of the factory." He rolled her chair out and fit his hand under her elbow. "Come on. I've already spoken to your supervisor. She knows."

Meg found Mrs. Xavier across the room standing at the fax machine. The woman nodded and waved her assent.

Leaving the business office, Meg asked if there was any-·thing in particular Curt wanted to see.

"Not really." He grinned, slanting a warm look her way. "I just got here too early and couldn't wait until noon to see you."

Meg stopped breathing, afraid that he meant what she *thought* he meant. "Well, let's start with the design studio, then."

They toured the entire plant, from the studio where jewelry designs were first conceived, down to the shipping room where the final product got packed for delivery. In between they had a lengthy visit on the assembly floor where most of the jewelry was still put together as it always had been, by hand, by sharp-eyed, deft-fingered women.

"How long did you say you've been working here?" Curt asked as they were making their way to the front entrance. She'd timed the tour well. Her watch read two minutes after twelve.

"Four and a half months."

"Four and a half months," Curt repeated, shaking his head. "How'd you learn so much in so short a time?"

She raised her hands, palms up. "I just find the industry fascinating." Was it that, she wondered, or a certain figure in the industry?

"Is there anything else I can do for you before we leave?"

"No. I do want to place another order," Curt said, opening the door for her, "but that can wait until we get back."

Meg recommended a restaurant downtown that overlooked the new riverwalk. She'd never eaten there but had read good reviews about its food. And the view was superb.

"I can't get over this city," Curt said, gazing out the window by their table. "It's changed so much in the past few years."

"This—" Meg lifted a hand toward the view "—is the result of the most ambitious urban renewal project ever undertaken in all of America." She smiled proudly. "Isn't it beautiful?" The weather was mild for late September, and the new canal through which the Providence River flowed was busy with kayaks and paddleboats. The walkways on either side were crowded, too, with lunch-hour pedestrians. So were the eight graceful bridges that lent the city a European look.

"I understand the river was moved during the project?"

Meg accepted a menu from their waiter. "Actually it was three rivers—the Providence, the Woonasquatucket and the Moshassuck. It was quite a feat of engineering."

"Not to mention of elocution."

They both laughed companionably.

"Oh, look! Here comes a gondola!" Meg pointed to one of the exquisite boats that could be hired to tour the canals, complete with gondolier dressed in slim dark pants, striped shirt and wide-brimmed hat, similar to the outfits worn by gondoliers in Venice.

After the waiter had taken their orders, Meg continued, "I love all the new construction, but I love the old better. Sometimes I spend my whole lunch hour just walking, admiring the architecture."

Curt smiled, his attention riveted on her. "What do you like best?"

She didn't have to think twice. "The East Side. Benefit Street especially." The waiter returned with their drinks, a club soda for Meg, a dark ale for Curt. "I read somewhere that it's the largest and most well-preserved district of Colonial and Federal architecture in the entire United States."

"That right?"

"Uh-huh. When I'm walking those narrow cobblestone streets, I can't help feeling I've been transported to another age."

Curt was leaning on his fist, staring at her, a bemused smile curving his mouth. She grew self-conscious.

"What? Am I babbling?"

Curt shook his head fractionally. "I'm just enjoying your enthusiasm. Do continue."

She did, but her thoughts had turned inward. Why was she here? she wondered for the umpteenth time. Why had Curt Forrest brought *her* to lunch?

Their food had arrived and they were well into it when she finally got her answer. "Meg, I spoke with my cousin Tina yesterday. She told me about you and Nathan, that you're not really dating."

Meg had a pretty good inkling where this was going. She tried to stall. "I guess I owe you an apology, too. Maybe I should just write up a group letter and send it to ev—"

Curt placed a finger over her lips and shook his head. "My only regret is that I didn't know sooner." His meaning couldn't have been clearer. "I'm not one to pussyfoot, so I'll just come out and ask it. Are you seeing anyone else?''

The feeling that her life was changing deepened immeasurably. She felt like the river outside their window. She was on the move, her life fluid, tumbling headlong into new realms. "No, I'm not seeing anyone else."

The corner of Curt's mouth flicked upward. "I'm going to be in the area through the weekend, Meg. Would I be disappointed if I asked you out while I was here?"

"Yes, probably." Meg watched his face drop and was sorry she'd tried to be cute. "What I mean is, I have a three-year-old daughter at home. I hope Tina also mentioned her."

As fast as Curt's disappointment had come on, it vanished. "Oh, if it's just a matter of baby-sitting, I can adjust my plans so we can include her. And, yes, Tina did mention her—Gracie, right? I've been dying to meet her ever since. I love kids. Tell me all about her."

Their conversation was animated, and it hardly abated as they left the restaurant. Curt was easy to talk to, comfortable to be with. He was also a boost to Meg's ego. By the time they arrived back at the factory, she'd agreed to meet him for dinner that evening.

"We'll go someplace casual, someplace with a play area," he said, "so Gracie can enjoy herself and give us a chance to talk."

Meg didn't know how *not* to accept such an accommodating invitation. A part of her didn't want to, either. Derek had been gone three years. It was time she started dating. Curt would make that difficult transition easy, too. She only wished she felt more of an attraction to him, but feelings of that nature were all tied up these days in someone else.

She didn't know what she could do about her attraction to that someone else, though. Nathan had made it clear he was a lost cause as far as romance went. Consequently, when Curt asked if she'd try to get a baby-sitter for Saturday night, she agreed to that, too.

"I've been wanting to attend WaterFire since I heard about it a year ago," he explained. "But the crowds and the late hour might be too much for Gracie."

"I agree." The elevator doors at the factory opened and Meg stepped in.

"Besides," Curt added on a grin, "I've already hired a gondola."

Meg swiveled, her lips parted in surprise. "You have?"

"Yes. And I've only made reservations for four."

The doors opened on the top floor, but Meg was too numb to move. "Four?"

"Mm. You and me, Nathan and whoever," he answered casually, stepping off.

She made herself follow. "Does Nathan know?"

"He knows this is the weekend I planned to be in the city. The gondola's a surprise, though." He noticed her hesitation. "I hope you're not going to feel uncomfortable out on the town with your boss along."

Meg capitalized on the ready-made excuse. "A little."

"Just ignore old Nate. If I know him, he'll be ignoring us." Curt seemed disinterested in discussing his cousin's role in his weekend plans any further. He moved on, instead, to the matter of placing another order.

A few minutes later Meg was sitting at her computer, entering serial numbers and other data pertinent to that order. She was also aware of the close attention Curt was paying her. He appeared to be taking note of not only her office skills but also her ready knowledge of prices and product.

After he left, Mrs. Xavier sidled over to Meg's work station. "What was that all about?"

Meg shook her head. "I wish I knew."

By dinnertime the following night, she did. That was when Curt offered her a job.

Nathan was standing at the door to his office when Meg stepped off the elevator on Friday morning. As soon as her gaze fell on him, her heart began to sing. The factory had felt empty with him gone. The very city had seemed abandoned. But suddenly all was right with the world once again. More than right. Gazing at Nathan, his silky black hair falling rakishly over his brow, Meg felt a rush of happiness so intense she grew scared.

He looked up from the newspaper he was reading, and a reaction seemed to course through him as well. He stood taller, his mouth softened, his eyes crinkled with a smile.

With a slight motion of his head, he gestured for her to join him in his office. She moved forward on legs drained of strength.

"Good morning," she said, trying to even out her breathing. "Did you have a good trip?"

Nathan closed the door. "Yes. I'm glad to be home, though." He placed a hand on her back, but instead of leading her further into the room as he'd obviously intended, he simply stood there a moment, gazing at her, his hand moving in slow, ever-lengthening strokes along her spine.

Oh, Nathan, what are you doing? she wondered, as his touch set off a shower of shivers over her skin.

He took a breath and looked away. "Come have a seat, Meg." He walked her to the chair by his desk where she usually sat and after pouring two cups of coffee, buzzed Mrs. Xavier to report that Meg would be detained. "So, how've you been, Maggie Mae?" he asked with a smile, settling comfortably in his big leather chair.

"Okay," she replied with difficulty. Something about his attitude toward her had changed.

"Tell me about your week, all of it." He lifted his coffee cup to his lips. She followed the movement with her eyes, feeling a reaction in the pit of her stomach. It took effort to marshal her thoughts.

Once she got them in hand, though, she filled him in on all the latest developments in her life—buying a car, dealing with the Department of Motor Vehicles, ordering contact lenses, opening an account at Sears. At his request, she also described Gracie's latest activities in school. He soaked up her words like a man thirsting for water.

She knew she'd eventually have to tell him about Curt. But since she was at a loss as to how to do that, she put it off a little longer.

"Well, sounds like your affairs are really coming together."

"Yes. It'll still be a while before I can think about getting an apartment. But you're right, other things are falling into place." She smiled, groaned and gave an exaggerated shiver, all at the same time.

Nathan laughed. "What's the matter?"

"It's scary, all these changes. Maybe not for someone like you, but I've never done any of this stuff before. Lord knows I've wanted to. I was prepared to take on the world when I was eighteen and first working. But then I met Derek, and before I could blink…" She let the rest of her sentence trail off.

"Well, the important thing is you're on the move now," Nathan said.

She sighed, setting down her empty cup. "Yes, I suppose."

He opened his briefcase and lifted out a small box. "While I was at the trade show I wandered a bit and found something I had to bring back to you." He extended the box to her.

"This is for me?"

He nodded, his face cautiously expectant as she took the box and lifted the cover. It was a watch. At first glance it appeared to be for a child, but it was clearly adult-sized.

"Oh, it's a Mary Engelbreit! I love her drawings." Smiling, Meg examined the illustration on the face of the watch more closely. It was a typical Engelbreit tot, with a hobo pack on his shoulder, walking past a crossroads down a long winding path. The caption encircling the picture read, Don't Look Back.

Meg's eyes shot to Nathan's, her throat tightening.

"You can do anything you want, Maggie Mae," he said softly. "Anything you set your mind and heart to." He stood up and helped her fasten the watch around her wrist. "Whenever you begin to doubt that, you just look at this little guy, okay?"

Meg swiped at her eyes. "Thank you."

"You're most welcome." Nathan turned and reached for a memo pad. "I just spotted this note when I was opening my briefcase. My cousin Curt's in town?"

Tension jerked Meg out of her sentimental mood. "Uh, yes. That was the next thing I was about to tell you. He came into the factory two days ago to place another order."

"Hmm. I didn't expect him until Saturday." Nathan scowled over the note. "Says here I can reach him at the Biltmore." He sighed. "I suppose I'll have to give him a call and make arrangements to meet him for dinner tonight."

Meg lowered her eyes, wondering how she'd gotten into such a bind. "I believe he's already made arrangements."

Curt glanced up sharply. "With whom?"

She gulped. "Me."

Nathan settled back into his chair slowly, as if every centimeter he traveled required the utmost caution. "You?"

She nodded. "But I'm sure he'd love to include you,

too. We were planning on someplace casual, so Gracie wouldn't get antsy."

"Gracie, too?"

Her throat kept tightening, making it hard to breathe. "Yes."

Nathan's jaw was rigid, his eyes dark and angry. "When did all this come about?"

"Wednesday." *Please don't ask me how,* she prayed.

"Could you tell me *how* this came about?" he asked.

Feeling like a condemned woman heading for the gallows, she told Nathan about the factory tour and lunch and meeting Curt for dinner. Nathan sat through it all quietly, but Meg felt she was trapped in a room with a gathering storm. His scowl was as dark as a thunderhead.

"Let me guess," he said finally. "He's asked you to go out with him tomorrow night, too."

Meg bit her lip to keep it from trembling. "Yes. But I believe he's thinking of it more as a group excursion. He's expecting you to be along, too."

"How thoughtful," Nathan shot back dryly.

Meg didn't have the courage to tell him he was expected to bring a date. "I'm not too sure what Curt's planning. Maybe you should call him for the details."

"Oh, I plan to," Nathan threatened, rising out of his chair. Meg realized he wanted her to leave.

"Wait," she said. "There's one more thing you ought to know."

Nathan thrust his hand through his hair which was already thoroughly tousled. "What more could there be?" he muttered, dropping into his chair again.

Meg's hands shook as she adjusted her glasses. "He's offered me a job."

"What!" Color rose through Nathan like mercury in a thermometer.

"I didn't accept it," she said quickly.

"Did you turn it down?"

She grimaced. "I told Curt that was likely."

"Which means you're still thinking about it. Great." Nathan's gaze slid away from her in disgust. "What's he offering?"

"Almost twice what I make here."

"And where would you be working? The Boston store?"

"No. At corporate headquarters."

If Nathan got any redder, she thought worriedly, he was going to have a stroke.

"In Brooklyn?"

"Yes. He plans to tell you all about it himself. He wants to be totally aboveboard so there won't be any hard feelings."

Nathan laughed, one great caustic bark. Then he rose from his chair and came around his desk. Before he could hoist her bodily, she gathered up her purse and shot to her feet. "Please don't be angry. I'm not plan—"

"I've heard enough." He gripped her arm and hurried her to the door. Tension emanated from him like sparks from a short-circuited wire. "It's time to get to work."

"Thank you again for the watch," Meg stammered.

He merely grunted before closing the door.

Nathan paced like a caged bear while the call went through to Curt's hotel room.

"Yes?" Curt answered.

Without preliminary conversation, Nathan exploded, "Boy, it didn't take *you* long!"

"Hey, Nathan!"

"Don't *Hey, Nathan* me. You've got some explaining to do."

"What the devil's got into you?"

"As if you don't know. You! You moving in on Meg while I was away. That's what's got into me."

"Whoa. I'm confused here, pal. I heard you and Meg were only pretending to be involved that weekend at your parents. I heard it from three different people, including Meg herself. Are you trying to tell me they were all lying?"

"No…"

"All right then. So, seeing how there was nothing going on, I figured you wouldn't mind if I took her out."

"You figured that, huh?"

Curt was silent a moment. "Are you telling me there *is* something going on?" Before Nathan could muster an answer Curt continued, "I asked Meg specifically if she was seeing anyone and she said no."

Nathan recalled the things he and Meg had done together. Dinner with his parents. That wasn't exactly a date. Walking around a used-car lot. Hardly what he'd call romantic. And intentions didn't count. He didn't have a leg to stand on, trying to lay claim on her romantically.

Knotted with frustration, he took a different tack. "You misunderstand. I'm just wondering what *you're* up to, that's all. Is this some sort of game? You know, competition for competition's sake?"

"How could it be when you're not involved? No, I really like Meg."

"She isn't your usual type, Curt." Usually when Curt visited, Nathan arranged dinner or theatre dates for the two of them, drawing on his select circle of female acquaintances, sophisticated women he knew from the country club, charity events, business and political dealings.

"Maybe my type has changed," Curt replied, sounding infuriatingly sincere. "Maybe it's age, but I'm not interested in flashy short-term stuff anymore. It bores me out of my gourd."

A wave of heat scorched its way through Nathan's body, leaving him weak in its aftermath. "You're thinking of Meg as someone long-term?"

"It's too early to say for sure. But the possibility is there. It's definitely there."

"Is that why you offered her a job in Brooklyn?"

"She told you about that, huh?" Curt had the grace to sound at least somewhat sheepish. "I was hoping to broach the subject with you in person."

"Well, you've got my ear now. Explain." Here finally was an area where Nathan could be safely angry.

"I see a lot of potential in her, Nathan, potential that could blossom in a more challenging environment, one with executive possibilities. I thought I'd make an offer before she got too entrenched at Forrest Jewelry. Again, I didn't think you'd mind, since she's only been with you a couple of months."

"A couple? Try almost five."

"Okay, almost five. I thought the move to Brooklyn would be good for her, too."

"What do you mean?"

Curt's sigh was long and eloquent. "Have you met her mother-in-law, by any chance?"

Nathan dropped into his chair, his anger slipping. "Quite a piece of work, isn't she?"

"I'll say. I took Meg and Gracie out for supper yesterday. The minute I returned them home, Vera came over, parked herself on the couch and started telling me stories about her son. When she threatened to go home for a photo album of baby pictures so I could see how much Gracie looks like him, I bolted."

"My bet is that was exactly what she wanted."

"I know. I called Meg later to ask about it and caught her crying. She tried to deny it, but...I eventually got her to tell me what was wrong."

Nathan dropped his head in his hand, plowing his fingers into his hair. His insides were twisting. That was *his* place—getting Meg to unload her troubles.

Curt continued, "After I left, Vera laced into Meg about all the gallivanting she's been doing, out with a different man every night of the week. Dragging her daughter along, too. Those are her words, of course."

Nathan swore under his breath.

"She told Meg she was bringing shame on their house and Derek's memory, and all the neighbors were talking."

"Son of a—"

"Yep. Did a real good tune on her. But that's not all. She'd already agreed to baby-sit tomorrow. Meg's supposed to go to Boston with your sister during the day, then at night there's WaterFire. But Vera withdrew her offer. Said she refuses to contribute to the shame. She also told Meg she belonged at home, not—get this—not out with a couple of rich playboys who only have one thing on their mind."

Nathan growled. "How many years do you think I'd get if I strangled that woman?"

Curt chuckled. "Tell you what, I'll share them with you."

"Thanks. So is Meg going to have to stay home tomorrow?" Maybe *he* could take care of Gracie during the day. He wanted Meg to enjoy the outing his sister had planned. He wouldn't baby-sit at night, though. Uh-uh. No way. Curt would just have to find another date.

"Nope. Meg found a baby-sitter. An ex-nanny, no less."

"Great," Nathan said although his enthusiasm was conflicted.

"Anyway, that's why I think moving away from here would do her good—aside from the job, aside from our personal relationship. That mother-in-law of hers just won't let go."

Greatly subdued, Nathan turned his chair to look out over the city. "She told me she hasn't given you an answer. Is that correct?"

"Uh-huh. Actually, she warned me she probably *wouldn't* take the job. But I think she just feels guilty about quitting your place. I have a hunch she'd leave if you gave her your blessing."

Nathan was feeling more depressed by the minute. He didn't want Meg feeling beholden to him. Grasping at the very last of his anger, he said, "Are you waiting for me to say I will? Sorry, Curt. Meg's going to have to make up her mind all on her own."

"But you won't try to dissuade her, either, I hope."

Nathan wanted to, but he knew he didn't have the right. What could he give Meg compared to the package Curt was offering? There was no room for her to advance at Forrest. Agnes Xavier wouldn't be retiring for another fifteen years, and Meg certainly wouldn't want to go out on the road as a salesman, which was the only other well-paying job he could see her filling.

Nathan couldn't match Curt on a personal level, either. A temporary relationship was all he could guarantee, whereas his cousin had no qualms about marriage, no hangups about kids. Just the opposite, Curt seemed eager to settle down.

Damn, he felt as if his insides were passing through a paper shredder, but if he wanted what was best for Meg there was only one answer he could give. "No, I won't try to dissuade her."

"Thanks. You're being bigger about this than I expected."

Don't count on it, Nathan thought.

"Now, how about tomorrow night? You're still going to join us, right?"

Nathan scowled. "You want *me* along? With you and Meg?"

Curt laughed dryly. "I thought you might consider bringing a date of your own."

"Oh. Oh, of course." Nathan grimaced. Double-dating with his cousin and Meg was the very last thing he wanted to do. But if he didn't go, they'd think he was hurt, angry, feeling betrayed and abandoned. And, dammit, even if he was, he had his pride. "Sure, I'll join you. Where do you want to meet?"

After discussing arrangements, Nathan hung up the phone and immediately reached into his left-hand drawer for his little black book. Yes, he'd join Curt and Meg for a night out. No reason why he shouldn't and every reason why he should.

Knowing Meg's best interests rested in accepting Curt's offer was a mighty bitter pill to swallow, however, he thought, thumbing the well-worn pages. He'd better find a mighty big spoon of sugar to help that pill go down.

CHAPTER NINE

AT NINE sharp on Saturday morning Meg arrived at the park-and-ride near the highway where Tina had asked to be met. As soon as the two other bridesmaids arrived and introductions got made, they piled into Tina's car and were off.

Though conversation was lively, Meg's thoughts returned continually to Gracie. The Gilberts had abruptly changed their mind yet again about watching her, once they realized Meg had an alternative baby-sitter. In fact, they'd insisted on it. They wanted to take Gracie to New Hampshire for two days—the same excursion Meg had proposed a few weeks earlier.

Lord, she hoped Gracie had a good time. Meg had felt uneasy saying goodbye to her this morning. Vera still seemed angry at Meg's going off today "gallivanting," more angry than eager for a trip to the mountains. But then, maybe that was just Meg's imagination.

Boston was only a forty-five minute drive away, but by the time they'd battled traffic and found a parking garage, it seemed half the morning was gone.

Tina caught Meg glancing at her watch. "Don't worry, I'll have you back in plenty of time for your big date. And just think how snazzy you'll look."

There *was* that, Meg thought. But that idea had been with her from the moment she'd realized Nathan would be along tonight and he'd be bringing someone. If Meg wasn't to fade completely into the background, she'd need professional help.

And if ever there was a place to get it, Newbury Street

was it. Among the myriad boutiques, art galleries and antiques stores, were dozens of salons. Striding along with the three other women, Meg began to feel hopeful, even enthusiastic.

"I thought we'd start here," Tina said, bringing her party to a halt at the steps of a day spa. "A massage. A session in a whirlpool or sauna. An herbal wrap for the skin. Any objections?"

"Are you kidding?" Tina's friend Claire exclaimed. "Bring it on!" She was the oldest of the party and the most outgoing. The fourth woman, Rene, was Meg's age and rather shy.

Meg had never been to a spa before, so she had nothing to compare this one to. But it seemed quite luxurious. They met with a personal hostess who plied them with herbal tea and escorted them to private dressing rooms where they changed into robes as thick and fluffy as clouds. New-age music and a soothing aroma accompanied them everywhere. Meg was relaxed before she even stepped into the massage room.

By the time she came out she was a puddle of contentment. Muscle spasms in her back, stiffness in her arms and legs—all gone. Even a headache she'd felt coming on this morning had vanished.

The women agreed to skip the sauna and went straight to having their skin treated—deep-cleansed, exfoliated, soothed and nourished. From the table next to Meg's, lathered in fruity green goop and with tea bags over her eyes, Claire laughed on a satisfied sigh. "This is so decadent it's sinful. I love it."

They stayed on at the spa for lunch—yogurt and fruit salad served with "health shakes" guaranteed to energize them all day. Meg and the three other women left the spa glowing.

From there they walked up the street to a hair salon. Meg

hadn't been to a salon in years. She'd just let her hair grow and grow, pinning it up for work to get it off her face. Even today she had it caught and anchored in a loose twist.

When she let it down, the stylist's eyebrows rose. "What do you have in mind?" he asked cautiously.

"I'm not sure. I just know I don't like *this.*" She flipped up a long limp lock.

The stylist, who'd introduced himself as David, nodded. "More isn't always more." He folded his arms, head cocked, studying her. "Let me play with it a while, get to know it."

Meg had never met a hairdresser who'd wanted to get to know her hair. "Trust him," Tina called from two chairs away. "David's a genius."

Meg shrugged on a nervous giggle. "Okay. Hair, this is David. David, meet my hair."

After nearly twenty minutes of brushing, lifting, ruffling and fingering her hair, David came up with a plan. "Considering the shape of your face, I think we should take about five inches off the bottom, bring it up to shoulder length, then cut long layers into the sides and add some wispy bangs."

He went on to explain why, mentioning her "delicious" cheekbones and "dramatic" jawline and her "big, beautiful" eyes. "They need to be framed properly," he said. "Attention brought to them." By then, Meg probably would've agreed to let him shave her head clean.

After he'd cut off the bulk, he sent her to a technician who gave her a penetrating hot-oil treatment. Once her hair was thoroughly conditioned, he resumed the cut.

Meg loved the result. She looked like a different person. But David had one more suggestion. Highlights.

"Highlights? Oh, I'm not sure I want to dye my hair."

"It isn't a full dye job. The effect will be subtle. Selected strands here and there just to warm and brighten your natural color."

"Go for it," the shy member of their party encouraged. Glancing down the length of mirror, Meg noticed that Rene was following her own advice. Her head bristled with permanent rods.

Meg threw up her hands. "Sure. Why not?"

David smiled and escorted her to a colorist's station.

From the hair salon, it was a short walk to the cosmetologist's. "Tina, this is getting a bit expensive, don't you think?" Claire commented on the way.

"Yes, but you see, my father loves me dearly and likes to see me happy. He also happens to be stinking rich. So, stop agonizing and just enjoy it."

Like the other places they'd visited, the cosmetics salon was sumptuous and took extra measures to serve its clientele. Before having her makeup done, Meg sat with a specialist who carefully studied her coloring—hair, skin and eyes—then educated her to "her" colors, the ones she should choose when buying makeup, clothing, and even jewelry. Meg was surprised to learn the shades she should have been avoiding. Many of them blighted her closet right now.

The cosmetologist, named Janine, then escorted her to a makeup station and went to work. She approached the job like an artist, preparing her "canvas" first with moisturizer, then selecting just the right base. She even had a special base for Meg's eyelids.

Then came the defining strokes: brow pencil, eyeshadow, liner, mascara, blush, lip liner, lipstick, setting powder. Janine applied more products than Meg had realized existed. Yet the result wasn't the mask she'd feared. Meg gazed at her reflection and clearly saw herself, but vastly improved. Her lips were full and defined. Her skin was vibrant and velvety. And her eyes…oh, her eyes. Even she could see how deep and mysterious they appeared.

"Hey," she laughed. "I look pretty good."

"Honey, you look great," Janine said. "Now, would you like to have your nails done?"

By 4:45 Meg was back home and staring at herself in the bathroom mirror. She was dumbstruck. To think *that* person had been hiding in her body all along! She wondered what Nathan would think when he saw her.

Immediately she kicked herself for the thought. She hadn't done this for Nathan. She hadn't. Aside from an initial show of displeasure, he hadn't said a word to her about her seeing Curt or about Curt's job offer. She'd drift out of his life and not leave a ripple. He hadn't thought twice about finding a date for tonight, either. Why would Nathan care about how she looked, when he didn't care about *her?*

She gave her new vibrant appearance another once-over. This was about pride. This was about reprisal and saying, See what you're missing? With a soft moan she finally admitted, "Okay, this is about Nathan."

She glanced at her watch. Curt would be by to pick her up at seven. Ostensibly she was ready now, except for dressing. But she already knew there was nothing in her closet that would do.

WaterFire was hardly a dress-up affair. Mainly the evening got spent strolling along the riverwalk and sitting on the canal. Most people would be wearing jeans. But Curt had said they'd be meeting for a drink first, and somehow Meg didn't expect any woman Nathan dated to show up in jeans.

Meg had an idea of what she wanted to wear. A jacket and pants outfit that straddled the line between dressy and casual. Something that could go from cocktail lounge to sidewalk with equal ease. Something stylish, sophisticated and preferably in a shade of wheat. It wouldn't hurt if it happened to be on sale, too. Did such an outfit exist? And if it did, could she find it in the next two hours? Meg wasn't sure, but she was determined to give it her best shot.

Her new credit card had arrived in today's mail. She slipped it into her wallet, glanced at the caption on her watch—Don't Look Back—and headed out the door for the nearest mall.

Nathan checked his watch. Curt and Meg were late. Not by much, but it still bothered him. Where the hell were they? What were they doing?

Across the table, Tabitha Simms was polishing off her second Manhattan and beginning to slur her words.

Didn't matter. She was gorgeous and lots of fun, and she adored him. What more could a guy ask on a night such as this?

Suddenly Curt and his date appeared at the door—and Nathan's heart surged to his throat. Was that Meg? Couldn't be. Had something happened to change Curt's plans? Had he invited someone else?

They started forward, and Nathan saw it *was* Meg. But not his Maggie Mae. He gripped his old-fashioned glass and downed his drink in one gulp before rising to meet this stranger.

Introductions were made and they sat. He still couldn't take his eyes off her. Oh, Lord. This wasn't supposed to happen. Table-turning wasn't on the agenda. What had she done to herself? She looked so good! *Why* had she done this? For Curt? The green fires of jealousy began to burn in Nathan's belly.

"Doesn't Meg look great?" Curt said proudly after their drinks arrived. Not just proudly—he was gloating.

"Mm." Stubbornly, Nathan held his reaction in check. "You're not wearing your glasses, I see."

Disappointment flickered briefly across Meg's face. "Yes, I have new contact lenses." He felt like a jerk.

"How are you adjusting to them?" Tabitha inquired.

"I find them strange, slightly uncomfortable."

"I did too at first. It'll get easier."

While the women fell to talking, Nathan cast Curt a glance. Curt was scowling at him. Nathan slid his gaze away. So Meg looked good tonight. What was that to him? He had his own companion to admire, and she was every bit as attractive. As a mark of just how little he cared, Nathan reached for Tabitha's hand, resting beside her drink. Meg didn't even blink, just went right on talking. The simmer of annoyance in Nathan's belly rose to a boil.

"So, what's this WaterFire all about?" Curt asked. "All I've heard is that fires are lit on the river, and extraordinary music gets played, and it's an event not to be missed."

Nathan took a sip of his freshened drink. "It's actually considered a multimedia work of art, Curt. An *installation* is the term used."

"A work of art?" Curt raised one skeptical eyebrow.

"Oh, it is!" Meg said, her eyes lighting up so that Nathan saw a hint of his Maggie Mae shining through the sultry enchantress she'd become tonight. "It's the creation of one artist, Barnaby Evans. Of course, he has hundreds of volunteers helping him, but it's his idea. He selects all the music that's played, and it changes each WaterFire night so it's never the same."

"This is beginning to sound intriguing." Curt sat with his arm extended across the back of Meg's chair, his fingertips stroking the top of her jacketed arm.

Meg's eyes shot to Nathan, then quickly moved away. "It is. I've only been to it once. I brought my daughter, and even she was mesmerized. Sitting on the wall along the canal, I felt as if I was within a giant…gosh, I don't know…not exactly a sculpture. The experience comes at you on too many sensory levels. All I know is, the city felt different, transformed. Almost mystical. I felt different too. Serene. I kept experiencing a strange sense of wonder, staring into the heart of those fires, then looking up and around at the city. I see those buildings every day, yet they seemed magical. It touched me deep inside.''

Nathan noticed her gaze flick to him again, then flick away. Her color deepened. Eyes lowered, she murmured, ''I guess it's just something you have to experience for yourself.''

He wanted to say her insights were lovely and intelligent. He wanted to say *she* was lovely and intelligent, too. But Curt beat him to it.

''Well put, Meg. That's exactly what art is supposed to do.'' Then turning to Nathan and Tabitha, ''She's not only beautiful, she's brilliant too.'' He gave her a squeeze that turned Nathan's stomach. ''Well, I for one can't wait to see this…installation. Shall we get going?''

Meg rose from her seat, glad to be doing something other than trying to ignore Nathan. Every time she saw him, he looked more attractive to her. Tonight he was wearing a dark gray sweater with thin blue threads running through it that matched his eyes. It was the sort of sweater tailor-made for a woman to snuggle into.

The woman with him was predictably gorgeous, a statuesque blonde whose father was a well-known industrialist. From small comments that were made, Meg deduced that she and Nathan were well acquainted, although how well acquainted was a matter of conjecture. Had they ever slept together? And when he took her home tonight, would he stay till morning? Meg felt nauseous at the thought.

The smell of the fires, drifting up from the river, met them as they left the East Side bar.

''Mm. I love the smell of wood burning,'' Curt said, taking Meg's hand.

"Cedar and pine," she said. "That's the only kind that's used. What's great is, it's all reclaimed from old fence posts and fallen trees."

Laughing, Curt said, "Isn't she something?"

Meg tried not to grimace, but she thought he was laying it on a little thick.

Nearing the bottom of the hill, they passed a cordoned-off stretch of street where small dining tables were set up and cooks were grilling food—beef, onions, peppers—and stuffing it into thick sandwich rolls. The mouth-watering aromas mingled with the cedar smoke—a hint of the sensual experience Meg had been trying to describe back at the lounge.

A small jazz band was playing nearby. But as Meg and the others drew nearer to South Main Street, the music from the river drowned out the jazz.

"Oh, wow!!" Curt stopped in his tracks, dumbstruck, as the fires came into view. "Oh, *wow!*"

"Wait till you see it from a bridge," Meg said, pulling him along through the thick crowds with Nathan and Tabitha on their heels.

They made it to the College Street Bridge, arching gracefully over the water. Deep dusk had fallen. Below, in both directions up and down the center of the canal, fires burned in large raised braziers, their golden flames reflected in the water. It was a magical sight.

Contributing equally to the magic was the music that filled the air. It came from concealed speakers so that it seemed to be rising from the river itself. The selections were eclectic, often odd, and drawn from all over the world. The present one was Middle Eastern, casting an exotic spell over the scene.

Meg and her three companions lined up at the rail, gazing at the fires, the river and its other bridges, listening to the strange, otherworldly music and saying very little. Curt's *Oh, wow* had said it all.

A few kayaks went by, a few canoes, a water taxi. Then came a wood boat, drifting silently. Heaped with firewood, the sturdy boat was painted black. The fire tenders within it were dressed in black as well to draw as little attention to themselves as possible as they tossed logs into the braziers. Meg thought they added a unique element all of their own. They, too, seemed otherworldly, travelers on a mythic river.

The sound of a horse pulling a carriage on the street behind them broke the spell. They turned as a hansom cab went by, carrying two couples, with a liveried driver at the reins.

"That's a nice sound, don't you think?" Meg commented. "The clopping of horseshoes on a city street?"

"Maybe we can take a ride later," Curt suggested.

In silent accord they moved on, holding hands so they wouldn't get separated in the crowd of thousands who'd turned out. They walked along the riverwalk, crossed several bridges to see the spectacle from different vantage points, and eventually made their way to WaterPlace Park. Here, the canal widened into a one-acre basin with an amphitheater rising on one side where outdoor performances were held. In the near distance, rose the state capitol building, majestically lit.

A gondola was just being off-loaded when they arrived at the docking platform. Curt went ahead to confirm their reservations.

"I didn't think I'd like this, if you want to know the truth," Tabitha remarked to Meg as they were waiting to board. "But I'm getting excited. How about you?"

"I'd say I'm holding myself together pretty well, considering what I want to do is jump up and down and shout 'Yippee.'"

Tabitha laughed. Meg had thought she'd dislike this woman or feel uncomfortable around her. But she didn't. Tonight she felt attractive, confident and strong in her own right. There was no reason to feel catty or inferior when a person felt this good about herself.

With an attendant's help, they stepped into the gondola and took their seats, Meg and Curt on one padded bench, Nathan and Tabitha on another facing them. A picnic basket was set between them on a small table.

"Enjoy your ride," called the attendant, helping the gondolier pole away from the landing. Soon they were off, circling the one-acre pond.

There were braziers here as well, set in a circle. At the center, a dramatic fountain spouted high overhead, catching the gold of the fires in its spray. The music had changed a few times since their arrival. Now it was something with a bizarre dirge-like quality.

While Curt uncorked the champagne, Tabitha laid out crackers and cheese and grapes from the basket. When everyone had a glass in hand they clinked them together, sipped and sat back.

Meg couldn't sit still, though. She wanted to see everything, and she wanted to see it all at once: the fires, the showers of sparks flying from them, the gondolier on the stern plying his one long oar, the other boaters and their sometimes unusual craft, the stars peeking through the clouds, the people on the banks, the monuments, buildings, the bridges. And sliding under those bridges, how the music resonated! She wanted to feel the heat of the fires, smell the smoke, hear the crackle and spit of the logs and be carried away on the music...

The gondola had almost completed the portion of the canal that was lighted by the fires when she finally remembered to take another sip of champagne. Sitting back, she realized Nathan was watching her, and probably had been for some time. His eyes were fixed on her, golden flames leaping within their dark blue depths. Gone was the disinterest he'd been showing her since yesterday. In its place was a look so intense, it stole her breath. Her heart soared, singing *Yes, yes, yes!*

They passed the last brazier and drifted on a while over the dark river before the gondolier made a U-turn. Coming back, Meg noted that the music had changed again. Now it was something operatic. She didn't know opera, but she did recognize Luciano Pavarotti's rich tenor voice.

"I don't believe this," she gasped.

Curt refilled everyone's champagne flutes. "What don't you believe, sweetheart?" He settled with his arm around her again.

"The music."

"Oh, right. That's from *La Boheme*, I believe. Don't you like it?"

"It's perfect." Her eyes drifted to Nathan's again. "Just the right touch."

"You're right," Tabitha commented. "It's very romantic."

Curt added, "Like life becoming a movie, complete with soundtrack."

Only problem was, Meg was sitting with the wrong leading man. She wanted to be where Tabitha was. She longed to feel Nathan next to her, not Curt. Her longing grew so acute that tears stung her eyes, blurring the fires and the stars and the crowds on the walkways. Oh, God, what was she going to do with all the love she felt for this man? How would she endure another minute of this painful pretense?

Nathan sat forward, removing his arm from Tabitha's shoulder, ostensibly to cut another slice of cheese. In truth, he'd had about all he could take of this situation. And if this ride didn't end soon he was going to punch his cousin right in his big, fat nose, which, at the moment was nuzzling Meg's hair.

God, he wanted her. He felt hot all over just looking at her. The light of the fires was dancing in her seductress's eyes. And, dammit, he was seduced.

He knew Curt was offering her a terrific job. He knew it was a chance for her to get away from her stifling in-laws and make a new start. But he didn't care anymore. He couldn't let her go.

All around them echoed the lush sounds of a full orchestra and one of the world's greatest tenors, singing of love in the language of love. The night had grown voluptuous, an overload to the senses. His chest felt tight with the need to profess his love—in operatic proportions at the very least. Everything that was romantic in him was pressing toward the surface. He was ready to battle windmills, slay dragons...

"Nathan, honey, are you all right?" Tabitha placed her hand on his shoulder and pulled him back, studying his face.

"Uh, no. Yes. I'm fine. I just got caught up in the aria." And being the coward that he was, he sat back and draped his arm along the bench. But he didn't stop wanting Meg. And he didn't stop thinking the time had come to do something about it.

Eventually the gondola returned them to the docking ramp where another eager party waited.

"Care to look for one of those horse-drawn carriages now?" Curt asked the group.

Meg glanced at her watch, the one Nathan had given her. Only nine o'clock. How could she possibly say she wanted to go home? She caught Nathan pulling back the cuff of his sweater, too.

"If you don't mind," he said, "I'm going to be a party-poop and call it a night. You were right, Tab. I wasn't feeling well. I have a helluva headache."

"Oh, poor baby." She moved to rub his temple but he ducked away. "Would you like some aspirin?"

"No. Aspirin isn't going to cure what ails me."

Curt shrugged. "Oh, well. Meg and I will just have to take that carriage ride alone."

Meg groaned inwardly. "You know, I'm beginning to wonder if some flu bug isn't going around, some virus Nathan and I both picked up at work."

Curt hovered over her. "Aren't you feeling well, either?"

She shook her head, unable to meet anyone's eyes. "Would you mind if I called it a night, too?"

Curt swallowed his obvious disappointment and agreed to take her home.

A half hour later Meg was standing at her bathroom mirror, wondering if she'd ever be able to re-create the exact effect the cosmetologist had produced, once she washed off her makeup. She'd bought some of the products used and had received directions on what to apply where, but she was still reluctant to wash her face. She thought she knew how Cinderella must have felt with midnight approaching.

Suddenly there was a knock at her door. Her heart sank. Was Curt coming back? Had he seen through her excuse? Guilt flooded her. He'd arranged such a wonderful evening for them all, he hadn't deserved to be lied to. But she simply wasn't interested in him romantically, and prolonging the evening would've only given him false hope.

Maybe it was good that he'd returned. She'd intended to talk to him tomorrow. He was supposed to call to discuss the job offer before he left for New York. Maybe it was better to talk now and make her feelings perfectly clear.

Tying her bathrobe securely, she crossed to the door and

peeked out its small square of glass. Suddenly adrenaline
was racing through her blood, making her heart pound, her
head light. It wasn't Curt standing out there. The man on
the stairs was the man in her dreams, the man in her heart,
the only man she wanted to be with, tonight and always.

CHAPTER TEN

NATHAN was resting casually against the railing, legs crossed at the ankles, but there was nothing casual about his eyes when they fixed on Meg. "How are you feeling?" he asked.

"Much better," she replied. "And you?"

A slow sensuous smile spread across his face. "Completely recovered. Must be that new 24-minute bug that's going around."

Meg's breath shivered out of her as he pushed away from the railing, entered her apartment and shut the door, his gaze on her all the while.

"I...I'll just go get some clothes on," she stammered. She started to step away, but Nathan caught her by the wrist.

"You have clothes on."

Her pulse pounded under his fingers. Slowly he brought her wrist to his lips, letting her know with a smile that he knew what she was feeling. "I had every intention of talking first, taking it slow," he murmured, pulling her smoothly into his arms. "But the hell with talking." He folded her closer, his words feathering over her lips. "Suddenly this is a lot more important."

I've died and gone to heaven, Meg thought in a daze, when Nathan dipped his head and kissed her. His lips were warm, soft, with the lingering taste of champagne. Intoxicating. She gripped his sweater and held on for dear life as the kiss went on and on and she grew lighter and dizzier.

Just when she thought she might float clear off her feet,

he eased away. She opened her eyes slowly. He was just opening his. Their gazes met and melded with the tacit understanding, it was time to be honest about their desire for each other. It was time to give in.

One corner of his mouth lifted. ''Ah, Maggie Mae, my beautiful maddening Meg. What are we going to do about this?''

''About what?''

''This.'' He kissed her again, deepening the spell he'd woven around her from the moment she'd first laid eyes on him. When he finally broke away he was breathing heavily. ''Talk. We need to talk.'' He pressed his lips to the top of her head and took a few deep breaths. When he'd regained composure he put some space between them and led her toward the couch.

''Oh, I forgot, Gracie's gone for the weekend,'' he said with a nod toward the open bedroom door.

Before she could make anything of her vulnerability, he'd pulled her onto the sofa with him, tucking her close.

''If you only knew how long I've wanted to do this...'' he murmured. ''Tonight you simply pushed me over the edge. You look so incredibly...provocative.''

''Me?'' She thought she looked much better than usual. But provocative?

''Oh, yes. That's not to say this wouldn't have happened without—'' his eyes roamed ''—whatever you've done to yourself. I'd already planned to start seeing you before I returned from Chicago. Instead, I came back to find Curt had moved in.''

Nathan shrugged the shoulder she was resting on. ''Ah, well. So we lost a few days. Just assure me we won't lose any more.'' He lifted her so that their eyes met. ''For my peace of mind, for my sanity, tell me you're not going to accept Curt's offer.''

This truly was a magical night. Meg couldn't shake the feeling of drifting through a golden haze.

Nathan continued, "I realize that'd be asking you to give up a lot, so I'm willing to make a counteroffer."

Meg frowned, putting even more space between them. "What do you have in mind?"

"Forrest Jewelry has been growing at a fantastic rate, and I've been thinking of taking on more help, creating positions at the executive level. Would you consider staying if I offered you one of those positions? I'd match whatever Curt was offering to pay you."

That lazy, hazy feeling of drifting through a fog was gone. Now Meg felt she was zooming at warp speed. She opened her mouth but nothing came.

"Are you doubting you can handle it?" he asked. When she nodded, he smiled. "That's okay. I have enough confidence in you for both of us." He took her hands in his.

"But won't it cause hard feelings in the office, my being promoted to such an advanced position after working there so short a time?"

Nathan conceded the point. "You'd have to work as an executive assistant for a while, a halfway step between the business office and the boardroom."

Meg bowed her head and raised their linked hands to her lips. "I'm confused. I'm going to have to think about this."

"I know. There are advantages and fringe benefits inherent in a move to New York—advantages and fringe benefits I can't offer you. All I'm asking is that you consider the ones I can."

She raised her eyes to his. The fires that burned in their blue depths told her what he meant. Oh, what he did to her! She felt like a wax figure melting under his gaze.

She needed to take a breather, needed to look at his offer more objectively. Questions were crowding her thoughts, not least of which was, how would they manage this difficult juggling act of dating and working together? But the question most on her mind was, what exactly was her other role? Employee and…what?

But those questions burned away in the heat of his eyes, disappeared completely when he took her in his arms and kissed her again. His touch was light at first, his parted lips moving over hers, slowly, sensuously, savoring their texture and warmth. But then he angled his mouth over hers, deepening the kiss, making it a fiery exploration. She opened under him, welcoming the sweet invasion with a soft whimpering moan.

Slowly she slid her hands up his arms to his shoulders, to his neck, savoring every virile muscle along the way before plowing into the dark silk of his hair.

Heat built between them, a fine tension of desire tightening their muscles, making their pulses race, their breath a rapid, shallow thing. He tipped her back into the cushions of the couch, never breaking the seal of their kiss, and half covered her body with his.

Sliding his hand between them, Nathan undid the tie of her robe, opened it back, and with a catch in his breath, palmed one breast, then the other.

"Ah, Maggie, if I don't leave now, pretty soon there'll be no turning back," he whispered hoarsely, his teeth nipping her earlobe.

"I know, I know." Meg combed her fingers through his hair. "And if you're asking for my approval, I want you to know," she said, laying breathless kisses on the corners of his mouth, "that it would be okay with me." Okay? Every cell in her being was crying out for this man. Every cell knew he was right. *They* were right. This was *it*.

Nathan lifted his head a little, looked into her eyes. "It would?" He seemed surprised.

She framed his face with her hands. "Oh, Nathan, of

course!'' she whispered with a smile. ''Don't you know how much I love you?''

Meg knew she'd crossed a forbidden line as soon as she'd spoken. A stillness came over the man in her arms. Although he didn't move physically, she felt him withdraw. She wanted to die right then and there.

Nathan recovered quickly, however. ''I think you know there's nothing I want more than to stay the night with you. But I'm not sure that's such a wise decision.''

She nodded, gathering the remnants of her pride. ''The neighbors would really have something to talk about then.'' She sat back, closed her robe, ran a hand through her hair.

Nathan stood and drew her up into his arms. ''I'll dream about you, though.'' She didn't doubt he would, just not in the way she would like.

''Will you let me come by tomorrow and take you to brunch? Better still, how about coming over to my place and I'll make you brunch?''

Meg knew she was at a crossroads. She should put an end to their relationship now, before she got hurt. And she *would* get hurt, guaranteed. She understood Nathan's stand on marriage and family. Whatever he was offering was only temporary, a relationship that would last just until the fires of passion went out or something better came along.

But putting a deliberate end to sharing his company and affection was about as possible as stopping the tides. Yes, it would end, and yes, she'd be hurt, but in the meantime…ah, that glorious meantime…

''What time do you want me over?''

''Eleven?''

He kept her tucked to his side as he walked to the door. ''Our heads are bound to be clearer in the morning. It'll be a good time to talk about this.''

She nodded, swallowing the question on her tongue. She already knew what he wanted to discuss—setting parameters on their relationship. That was if she was lucky. After her foolish admission of love, he might want to end things altogether.

He kissed her one more time, and then left.

Meg was slipping on her nightgown when the phone rang. It was nearly eleven. Who on earth would be calling her now? she wondered. No one she knew—except maybe Nathan. "Hello," she said hopefully.

But as the person on the other end of the line conveyed his message, her smile faded and confusion took its place. It was a policeman, and he was telling her...Gracie had been hit by a car?

His words swirled, blurred, didn't make sense. Gracie was with her grandparents up north, Meg protested. She couldn't have been hit by a car. So he explained it again. He was a New Hampshire state trooper, and he'd escorted her daughter to a hospital outside Conway earlier in the evening. Slowly, his words began to sort themselves, understanding bringing with it a terror that set Meg to shaking.

As soon as she had all the details, she said, "I'll be right there. Well, as soon as I can. It's about a three-hour drive."

The officer told her to be careful on the road and not to worry, Gracie wasn't seriously injured.

"Yeah, right," she cried, tugging on her jeans. Within two minutes from hanging up, she was on the road.

Nathan was poking through his refrigerator, checking what he had on hand for tomorrow's brunch, when the phone rang. He glanced at the clock. It was eleven-thirty. Who the devil...?

"Nathan?" came a voice he barely recognized.

"Meg?" He filled with concern. She sounded so strange, her voice thin, tremulous. "What's the matter, sweetheart?"

"I'm calling to cancel brunch. I won't be able to make it."

"Oh, that's too bad." Nathan heard unfamiliar noises in the background. "Where are you?"

She sniffed. "At a rest stop on the highway. I needed to get a cup of coffee."

"What! What are you doing…?"

"Um…Gracie had an accident tonight. She was hit by a car."

The news struck him with the force of a bullet. "Oh, God. How serious?" *Please let her be okay. Please.*

"I'm not sure. The policeman I talked with said she's okay, but he might've just wanted me to stay calm so I could drive."

In the next moment Nathan felt the impact of another bullet. "Why didn't you call me right away, Meg?"

"Oh…it was late. And I just wanted to get on the road."

Nathan swore silently. "You should've called. You shouldn't be driving alone. How long *have* you been driving?" If she wasn't too far away, maybe he could overtake her.

"About thirty minutes. Don't worry. I'm all right, Nathan. I didn't call to worry you. I just didn't want you going to a lot of trouble tomorrow for nothing."

Nathan made a fist and pressed it to the wall, swearing again. He knew damn well why she hadn't called him. Because she didn't trust him to come through in a situation like this. Knowing how his wife and daughter had been taken from him, she probably thought he couldn't handle it. He didn't blame her. Had he ever given her reason to believe he could? Or *would?* Not in his recollection. A fair-weather lover—that's all he'd ever made himself out to be.

He gazed at his fist. Even pressed against the wall it was trembling. Maybe Meg was right.

"When did the accident happen?"

"About eight-thirty."

"And no one called until now?" Nathan's blood pressure zoomed.

"The Gilberts told the police I'd be out all evening."

Nathan heard a heavy dose of guilt in her voice. "It wasn't your fault, Meg. They could've left a message." Before she could protest, he asked, "Were the Gilberts hurt, too?"

"No. Gracie was alone."

"Alone!"

"Mm. Vera and Jay took her someplace tonight, and she wandered off. I…I don't fully understand it yet. But anyway, she was alone, walking along a road, and a car…" Her voice had been breaking up. Now it gave out altogether.

"That's okay, honey, you don't have to continue." Nathan pulled in a deep breath. "Where is she now?"

Meg named a hospital, then added anxiously, "I have a distance to go yet."

"Okay, I won't keep you. Drive carefully."

"I will. Oh, before you go, can I ask a favor? Will you call Curt for me and tell him the news?"

Nathan had thought he couldn't feel any worse about her lack of faith in him. He'd been wrong. Gritting his teeth, he said, "Sure."

"Thanks. He was going to call me tomorrow, but I'm not sure I'll be back." As if that was the only reason.

Even though it galled him, Nathan called Curt as soon as Meg hung up. He just wanted to deliver the news. He was in no mood to talk, but he did want to know if his cousin planned to drive up to the hospital.

"I'd like to," Curt replied. "But I won't. I know when I'm beat."

"What are you talking about?"

"Me and Meg. The chance of our ever getting together."

"How can you say you're beat when you're holding the trump card?"

"You mean, the job offer?"

"No. Your openness to marriage and having kids."

Curt chuckled sadly. "Simple. Meg isn't in love with me. The trump's in your hand, where it's been all along. Maybe one of these days you'll actually find the courage to play it."

And if he did, would Meg still be waiting? Nathan doubted it. Not after this. He hung up the phone scowling worse than thunder. He pictured her alone on the road, imagined the thoughts that must be going through her mind, the terror she must be feeling—and no one to share it with. When this ordeal was over, she was bound to realize she deserved better. After tonight, he wouldn't have a chance.

The drive to New Hampshire was the worst three hours of Meg's life, worse even than the hours she'd waited outside the ICU after Derek's accident. This was her daughter, her innocent baby. Knowing Gracie was hurt, but not how badly, was the worst torture there was.

On second thought, maybe it wasn't. Knowing Gracie was alone, without Meg there to comfort her, was worse. Whenever she thought about her daughter possibly being in pain and conscious, Meg became undone.

Of course Vera and Jay would be there, but no comfort came from that thought, only thoughts of how careless they'd been to let Gracie wander off. Meg would try to control her anger when she saw them, though. They were probably in worse shape than she was, worrying over Gracie.

And that was another reason Meg drew no solace from their being at the hospital. They might be overwrought, upsetting Gracie more than helping her. Meg *really* wasn't looking forward to confronting them if that was the case.

She didn't need a whole other set of problems to deal with, draining energy that could be put to better use elsewhere.

Meg drove on as fast as she dared. She didn't feel tired, but she knew that was just adrenaline. She *was* tired. It had been a long, busy day.

A thousand times during that drive she wished she had someone with her. No, not just someone. Nathan. She felt totally alone, and the night was so dark. She longed for his company, wished he was here to share her burden, lend her his strength.

She'd thought about calling him as soon as she'd been told the news, but immediately put it out of her mind. Nathan was still working on just being around kids. It wasn't fair to ask him to cope with a child in trouble. In fact, after tonight, she doubted there'd be anything left of their romantic relationship. This crisis was a vivid reminder of what he didn't want in his life anymore.

Finding her own strength, Meg pushed on. It was close to 2:00 a.m. when she finally dashed into the hospital's main lobby, legs weak, head light and dizzy.

"May I help you?" asked an elderly man at the information desk. His eyes flicked over her. She could only imagine what a fright she looked.

"Yes. My daughter was admitted earlier. A car accident. Last name's Gilbert." Meg realized she was hyperventilating. *Deep breaths, Margaret Mary. Deep breaths.*

The man checked his files. To Meg he seemed to be moving with the slowness of an underwater swimmer. Hurry, hurry, she thought.

"Ah, yes. She's in pediatrics, third floor, room 305."

"She's in a regular hospital room?"

"Yes. And resting comfortably." He smiled reassuringly.

Meg wasn't reassured, however. Hospitals always said patients were "resting comfortably." Had Gracie been through surgery? Was she resting because she was knocked out on painkillers?

"You can go right up and see her," the man said with a smile. "Elevators are that way." She thanked him and dashed off.

The elevator doors opened onto a softly lit lobby decorated with balloons and cartoon characters. It being the middle of the night, the floor was quiet, almost peaceful.

"Hi, I'm Meg Gilbert," she said to the young nurse at the desk.

"Oh, yes. We've been expecting you." In no particular hurry, the nurse came around the desk. "There's a police officer waiting to speak with you. He's in the lounge at the end of the corridor."

At that moment Meg couldn't have cared less about the legalities of the accident.

The nurse smiled. "But first things first." She started down the hall, Meg by her side.

"Is there a doctor with my daughter?"

"Not right now. Dr. Jeremy just went to check on another patient, but I'll tell him you're here."

They passed several rooms, doors partially opened, light filtering in and dimly disclosing small beds, small strangers—some in casts, some hooked to monitors. Meg's anxiety deepened until she thought her nerves would snap.

Almost to the end of the corridor, Meg noticed the lounge where the officer was sitting, hunched over a cup of coffee. Across from him sat Vera and Jay, slumped together, eyes closed.

She paused, staring in disbelief. "Is my daughter alone?" Her grief became so interwoven with anger she could barely tell the emotions apart. "Is *no one* with her?"

Before the nurse could answer, a deep familiar voice came to her from within the room behind her. "No, Meg, she isn't alone. I'm here."

CHAPTER ELEVEN

IT WAS one of those rare moments in life when the soul seems to leave the body and do a few spins in the clouds before resettling. Meg stared at Nathan—he was sitting by a sleeping Gracie, gently stroking her head—but she felt she was looking at him from another dimension.

"Mr. Forrest arrived about an hour ago," the nurse explained. "He's been a tremendous help." She glanced from Meg to Nathan. "But maybe I should leave you three alone for a while."

Still in a surreal fog, Meg tiptoed into the softly lit room. Gracie was hooked to an IV, and her forehead was bandaged. "Oh, God," she whispered, her jaw wobbling.

Nathan got up, came around the bed and wrapped Meg in a tight embrace, absorbing her tremors. "She's fine, Meg. The doctor will explain it in more detail, but the bottom line is she's fine."

Meg pulled back so that she could see his eyes.

He nodded. "I'm not lying. Her worst injury was a dislocated shoulder, and that's already been set. She has a nasty scrape on her head and some bruises that are going to be uncomfortable for a while, but other than that…"

"She was hit by a *car,* Nathan."

"Sideswiped, not hit. The driver saw her in enough time to swerve."

"Even so, she's so small. There might be internal injuries."

Nathan shook his head. "She's been thoroughly tested, X-rayed and scanned."

"And she's all right?" Meg still found it impossible to believe.

With an arm across her shoulder, Nathan turned her to look at the slumbering child. "You forget, she's an amazing child, our little Gracie."

Meg leaned over the bed and placed a soft kiss on her daughter's head. "I'd call this downright miraculous."

Nathan smiled. "I, for one, can use a miracle in my life right about now."

They stood for a long while gazing at the child, arms around each other's waist.

"Speaking of miracles," Meg said, casting him an arch look, "would you mind telling me how you happen to be here?"

"I flew, Meg. I have my own plane. If you had called me, you could've flown, too." A mild chastisement came with his words.

Meg lowered her eyes back to Gracie. "Was she sleeping like this when you arrived?"

"No, she was awake. Wide awake."

"How did she seem to you?"

"Not bad. The people tending her had assured her repeatedly you were on your way."

"Your tone is telling me she wasn't in good shape either. Oh, Nathan, was she frightened?"

Nathan shook his head. "No, she was tense. Apprehensive. Vera was a wreck, yet insisted on staying with Gracie. Nothing the nurses could do or say could pry her away."

"Until you got here?"

Nathan shrugged negligently.

"Thank you," Meg murmured softly. "Have you learned any of the details, like how she came to be walking along a road by herself?"

"Uh-huh. Gracie and I had a little chat before she went

to sleep.'' Nathan led Meg over to a pair of chairs by the window. One of them contained a large bear, which she instinctively knew he'd bought. He moved it to the floor and sat. ''She was trying to go home.''

''Home!''

''That's what she told me. Seems your in-laws were doing a lot of talking about you in her presence—as if she couldn't understand. Whatever they said, she interpreted as bad. *You* were bad. They also told her you were planning to take her away from them, but they wouldn't let that happen, ever. From what she said in her childish way, I figure the Gilberts were discussing a custody suit.''

''What!'' Meg felt rage in every particle of her being.

''Gracie thought they were taking her away from you already. So, minx that she is, she ran off while they were in a crowded toy store—buying her another bribe, I suppose. She would've been found soon; she hadn't gone more than a few hundred yards when the accident occurred. But, the long and short of it is, none of it should've happened at all.''

Meg slumped onto the arm of the chair, her head heavy in her hand. ''Oh, God! Am I going to be facing a custody fight now?''

Nathan gently massaged her tense neck. ''Of course not.''

''How can you be so sure?''

''Because I told them to back off, they don't have a leg to stand on.''

Meg stared at him, dumbfounded. ''And all this time I thought I was alone. I felt alone. But you were here, taking care of things all along.''

Nathan cradled her head against his shoulder, which helped muffle the sobs she was trying so hard to contain. ''Well, get used to it, Maggie Mae, because I intend to be here taking care of things for a very long time.''

Meg went still. Slowly she lifted her head, afraid to believe what she was hearing.

Nathan smoothed back her hair, a look of uncertainty entering his expression. "If you'll forgive me for being so slow, that is."

"Slow?"

He nodded. "Cautious. Even a few hours ago I was afraid to say I loved you. When I left your place I still thought we needed to talk, set rules and limits on what we could expect in a relationship. I wanted to wait, see what happened with us." His voice sank. "But then I got your call."

He swallowed with difficulty. "I felt so damn awful, knowing you'd taken off on your own because you thought you couldn't depend on me. I figured this was it, a defining moment for you. You'd realize you were wasting your time with me and deserved better. I learned instantly that there *is* no waiting for some things in life. So—here I am."

Nathan took her hands in his, brought them to his lips and kissed them. "I love you, Meg. I love you with all my heart. I love Gracie, too, and I'll spend as long as I have to, trying to prove it to you, if only you'll tell me we have a chance."

A tear slipped from Meg's eye. He brushed it away with his thumb.

"There's no need to prove anything, Nathan. You already have."

Nathan released an unsteady breath. He seemed to be making an effort to keep his jaw firm. Meg took him in her arms, holding him close.

"I love you so very much, Nathan. If you need to wait, I understand. I'll wait, too. For you, I can wait forever."

He pressed kisses to her hair, to her eyes, cheeks and chin, and finally to her lips. "No, there's no need. In fact, from here on—" he smiled with a touch of roguishness "—you'd better hang onto your hat, lady. You're way overdue to be romanced."

Meg laughed softly, bowing her head to his. But then she eased back, sobering. "I have one last question—just to clarify things. What exactly *will* our relationship be?'' She could feel herself growing warm with embarrassment. ''I mean, I know I'm your secretary, and I think I'm your friend, and you'd like me to be an executive assistant and…and your lover…'' She left the sentence open-ended.

Nathan framed her face in his large, warm hands, his eyes adoring. ''Will you please add wife to the list, Meg?''

''Wife?''

''Oh, yes. I won't be satisfied till you're my everything.''

Two weeks later, as planned, Meg served as a bridesmaid in Tina Forrest's wedding. She was paired up with Nathan, who was one of the ushers. Awash in flowers and candlelight, Beechcroft was resplendent—a perfect setting for a perfect ceremony.

But there was a last minute feature no one had anticipated—Gracie, attending as a flower girl. With her bouncing blond curls and winning smile, she stole the hearts of every last guest—even if, in her excitement, she forgot to toss a single petal.

Meg and Nathan had agreed beforehand to avoid talking about themselves. They wanted the spotlight to remain firmly on the bride and groom. But their happiness was obvious. So was the new engagement ring on Meg's left hand. With dinner over and the dancing begun, talk inevitably turned on them.

''So, what *are* your plans?'' Curt asked, lounging at the table where Meg and Nathan were sitting with some other family members. He was being a remarkably good sport about the whole thing. In fact, he was expending an unusual amount of energy pursuing Susan Corning. ''Are you still living with those—'' he cleared his throat ''—with the Gilberts?''

Meg nodded. ''And I will be for a while.''

Nathan continued, ''We want them to understand they're

not being abandoned. They'll always be Gracie's grandparents, and we'll make sure to visit often after we're married.''

"I expect they'll continue to do some baby-sitting, too," Meg added. "But I don't think it'd be appropriate for me to be married from their house. As soon as I see they're comfortable with me and Gracie moving out, Nathan is going to have a couple of houseguests."

Curt shook his head. "That's awfully generous of you, Meg, considering what happened on that trip to New Hampshire."

"Yes, well, they were pretty shaken by the incident, too. I think it woke them up to how clinging they'd become."

"A kind way of putting it," Curt cut in.

Meg shrugged. "Anyway, they've been much more reasonable about things lately. That's why I think it won't be long before I'll be moving out."

Pia Forrest sat forward avidly. "I don't mean to be rushing things, but have you two set a date yet?"

Her son laughed. "Of course you mean to rush things. But to answer your question, no, we have no firm date. We're thinking spring, though."

"Ah. Spring." Mrs. Forrest's eyes twinkled as they lifted and scanned the salon, presently festooned in autumn tones.

Tina laughed, setting her short tulle veil to shimmering. "Here we go again. Move over, Martha Stewart!"

"And to think," Mrs. Forrest said with a vindicated smile, "It all started because Nathan was trying to get out of being matched up. Ironic, wouldn't you say?" Everyone got a good laugh from that.

Gracie came running off the dance floor where she and a future cousin had been "waltzing."

"Mommy, come dance with me," she said, her flushed cheeks matching the rose-colored sash of her long chiffon dress.

"Can I join in?" Nathan asked.

"Oh, of course!" she said in such an adult manner, everyone laughed again.

Nathan lifted her onto his left arm, wrapped Meg in his right, then twirled his little family out onto the dance floor. He was impossibly happy, he realized. Only weeks ago, he'd thought this kind of happiness came only once in life. He'd considered himself a "lost cause." Somehow, though, that lost cause had been found—like in the hymn he sang to Gracie every night.

Recently he'd put away the last of the photographs from his old life. He'd packed them in a box in his parents' attic where they'd be safe but out of the way, just as his mother had urged him to do on so many occasions. It was time to make room for the new. Gazing down at his beautiful Meg, he had a hunch his present happiness was going to pale in comparison to what lay ahead.

"There we are!" Gracie exclaimed. "Look. In the mirror."

Meg gazed toward a seven-foot-tall, gilt-framed mirror, one of several in the room. "Oh, yes! I see."

"We're at the ball, Mommy. We're dancing with the prince."

Nathan and Meg laughed. Nathan *did* look terribly princely, decked out in his black tuxedo, Meg thought. She didn't look so bad herself, in her elegant bridesmaid's gown of wine-colored velvet. And this chandelier-lit setting did look fit for a fairy tale.

Still chuckling, Nathan pressed a kiss to Gracie's curls, then let his gaze link with Meg's. His amusement vanished, melting into adoration right before he touched his lips to hers.

But this wasn't a fairy tale, Meg thought. Perhaps her daughter couldn't tell the difference yet, but she could. Fantasy had become reality, and Meg couldn't have been happier. After all, there was nothing like the real thing.

MILLS & BOON®

Makes
any time
special

Enjoy a romantic novel from
Mills & Boon®

Presents...™   *Enchanted*™   TEMPTATION.

Historical Romance™   ⊣ **MEDICAL**
ROMANCE™

COMING NEXT MONTH

MILLS & BOON®

Enchanted™

THE NINE-MONTH BRIDE by Judy Christenberry

Susannah longed for a baby and Lucas desperately wanted a son, but not the emotional ties of marriage. So they decided to make a convenient marriage, then make a baby – the old-fashioned way…

THE BOSS AND THE BEAUTY by Donna Clayton

Cindy was determined to make her boss, Kyle, see her as a woman rather than his employee. But as Kyle *never* mixed business with pleasure—it was going to be a long haul to get this man from the boardroom to the altar!

TAMING JASON by Lucy Gordon

Jason was injured and temporarily blind, and for his sake Elinor must keep her identity a secret. What would happen when he was able to see her again – and recognise her as the woman he'd once considered unsuitable for marriage?

A HUSBAND WORTH WAITING FOR
by Grace Green

After his accident Jed's memory loss turned him into an entirely different man. Sarah found him charming—even seductive! But how long until Jed's memory returned? And when it did, would he still be a husband worth waiting for?

Available from 4th February 2000

COMING NEXT MONTH

MILLS & BOON®

Enchanted™

BORROWED BACHELOR by Barbara Hannay

Maddy needed a man who'd pretend to be her boyfriend,
and her sexy neighbour Rick seemed ideal. Yet Rick played
the part of the attentive lover so convincingly that even
Maddy's mind turned towards marriage…

MEANT FOR YOU by Patricia Knoll

Jed thinks Caitlin is too uptight. She thinks Jed is too laid-
back. All they have to do is stick to their separate sides of the
house. So why do they keep meeting in the hallway?

MARRYING MARGOT by Barbara McMahon

The worst time in Rand's life had been when he and Margot
had lost their baby and their young marriage had floundered.
Now Rand wanted a reconciliation and more children.
Margot still loved him, but she couldn't go through the
heartache again…

THE BILLIONAIRE DADDY by Renee Roszel

Baby Tina needed a mum and her aunt Lauren wanted to take
on the role—as soon as she had dealt with Tina's so-called
'father', Dade Delacourt. When Dade mistook Lauren for
Tina's nanny the mistake gave Lauren the ideal opportunity to
check out Dade's parenting skills. Except the plan backfired
because the irresistible billionaire expected her to be with him
twenty-four hours a day…

Available from 4th February 2000

2 FREE

books and a surprise gift!

We would like to take this opportunity to thank you for reading this Mills & Boon® book by offering you the chance to take TWO more specially selected titles from the Enchanted™ series absolutely FREE! We're also making this offer to introduce you to the benefits of the Reader Service™—

- ★ FREE home delivery
- ★ FREE gifts and competitions
- ★ FREE monthly Newsletter
- ★ Exclusive Reader Service discounts
- ★ Books available before they're in the shops

Accepting these FREE books and gift places you under no obligation to buy, you may cancel at any time, even after receiving your free shipment. Simply complete your details below and return the entire page to the address below. *You don't even need a stamp!*

YES! Please send me 2 free Enchanted books and a surprise gift. I understand that unless you hear from me, I will receive 4 superb new titles every month for just £2.40 each, postage and packing free. I am under no obligation to purchase any books and may cancel my subscription at any time. The free books and gift will be mine to keep in any case.

N0EA

Ms/Mrs/Miss/Mr ....Initials.....................................
BLOCK CAPITALS PLEASE

Surname ....

Address ....

....

....Postcode..................................

Send this whole page to:
UK: FREEPOST CN81, Croydon, CR9 3WZ
EIRE: PO Box 4546, Kilcock, County Kildare (stamp required)